jGNOV   17.95
MILLER, DAVIS
JOURNEY TO THE CENTER OF THE EARTH

JULES VERNE'S

JOURNEY TO THE CENTER OF THE EARTH

RETOLD BY DAVIS WORTH MILLER
AND KATHERINE MCLEAN BREVARD
ILLUSTRATED BY GREG REBIS
COLOR BY PROTOBUNKER STUDIO

Librarian Reviewer
Katharine Kan
Graphic novel reviewer and Library Consultant, Panama City, FL
MLS in Library and Information Studies, University of Hawaii at Manoa, HI

Reading Consultant
Elizabeth Stedem
Educator/Consultant, Colorado Springs, CO
MA in Elementary Education, University of Denver, CO

STONE ARCH BOOKS
Minneapolis San Diego

Graphic Revolve is published by Stone Arch Books,
151 Good Counsel Drive, P.O. Box 669,
Mankato, Minnesota 56002.
www.stonearchbooks.com

Library of Congress Cataloging-in-Publication Data
Miller, Davis Worth.
Journey to the Center of the Earth / by Jules Verne; retold by Davis Worth Miller and Katherine McLean Brevard; illustrated by Greg Rebis.
p. cm. — (Graphic Revolve)
ISBN-13: 978-1-59889-832-3 (library binding)
ISBN-10: 1-59889-832-9 (library binding)
ISBN-13: 978-1-59889-888-0 (paperback)
ISBN-10: 1-59889-888-4 (paperback)
1. Graphic novels. I. Brevard, Katherine McLean. II. Rebis, Greg. III. Verne, Jules, 1828–1905. Voyage au centre de la terre. IV. Title.
PN6727.M546J68 2008
741.5'973—dc22 2007006202

Summary: Axel and his uncle find a note that describes a path to Earth's center! The men climb deep inside a volcano and discover amazing wonders. They also run into danger, which could trap them below the surface forever.

Art Director: Heather Kindseth
Graphic Designer: Kay Fraser

1 2 3 4 5 6 12 11 10 09 08 07

Printed in the United States of America

TABLE OF CONTENTS

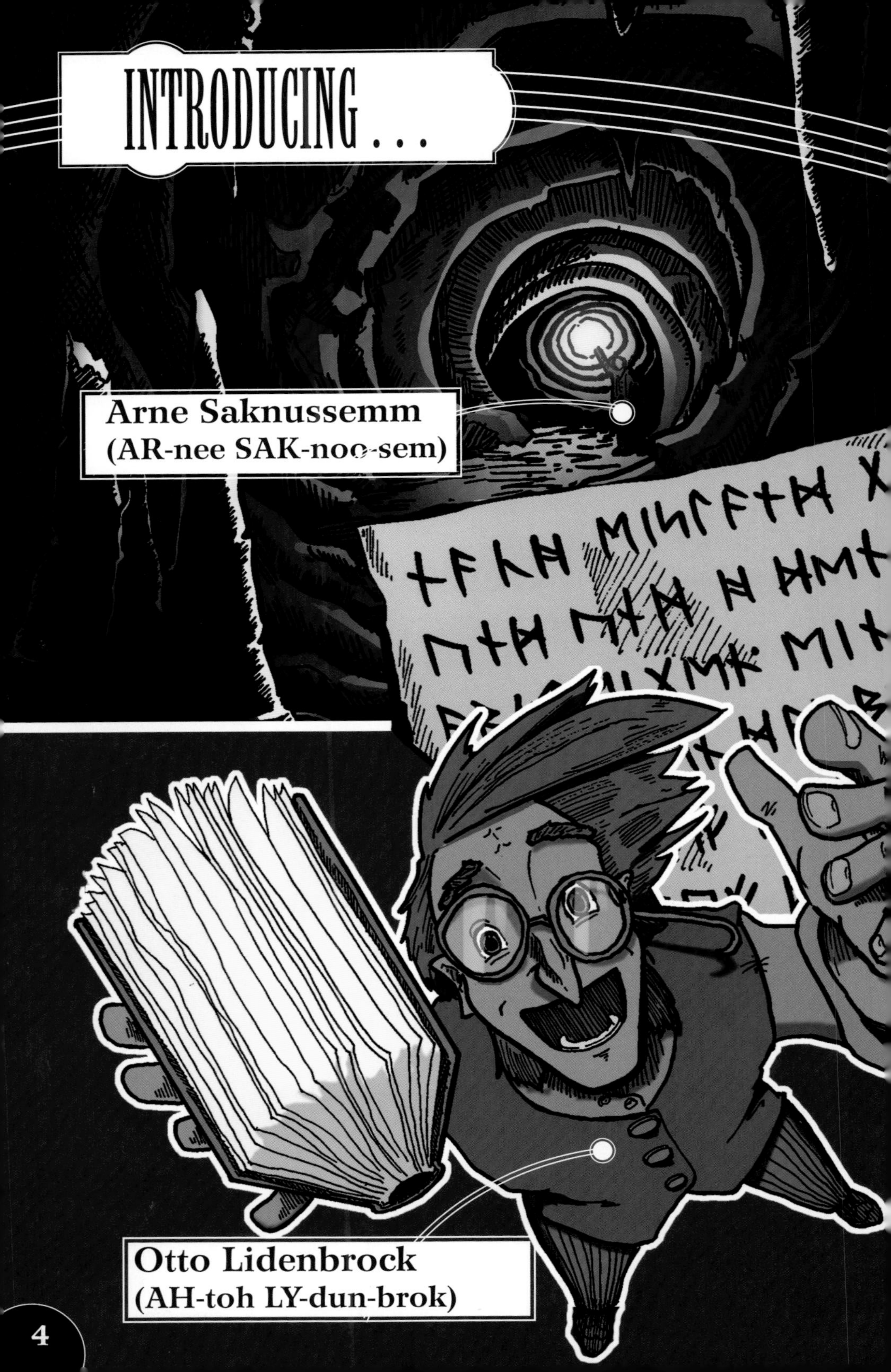
INTRODUCING . . .
Arne Saknussemm
(AR-nee SAK-noo-sem)
Otto Lidenbrock
(AH-toh LY-dun-brok)

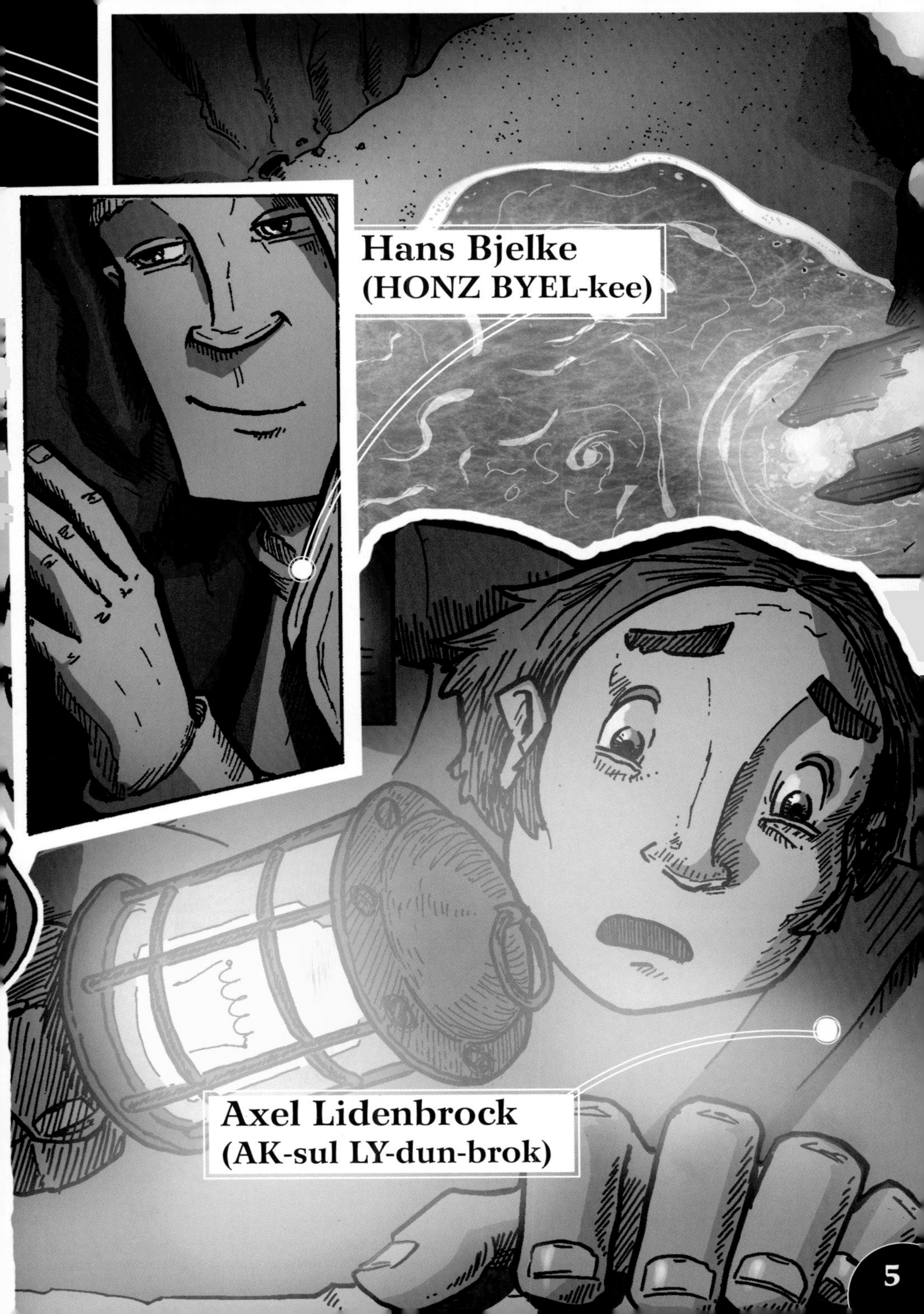
Hans Bjelke
(HONZ BYEL-kee)
Axel Lidenbrock
(AK-sul LY-dun-brok)

CHAPTER 1 A GREAT DISCOVERY

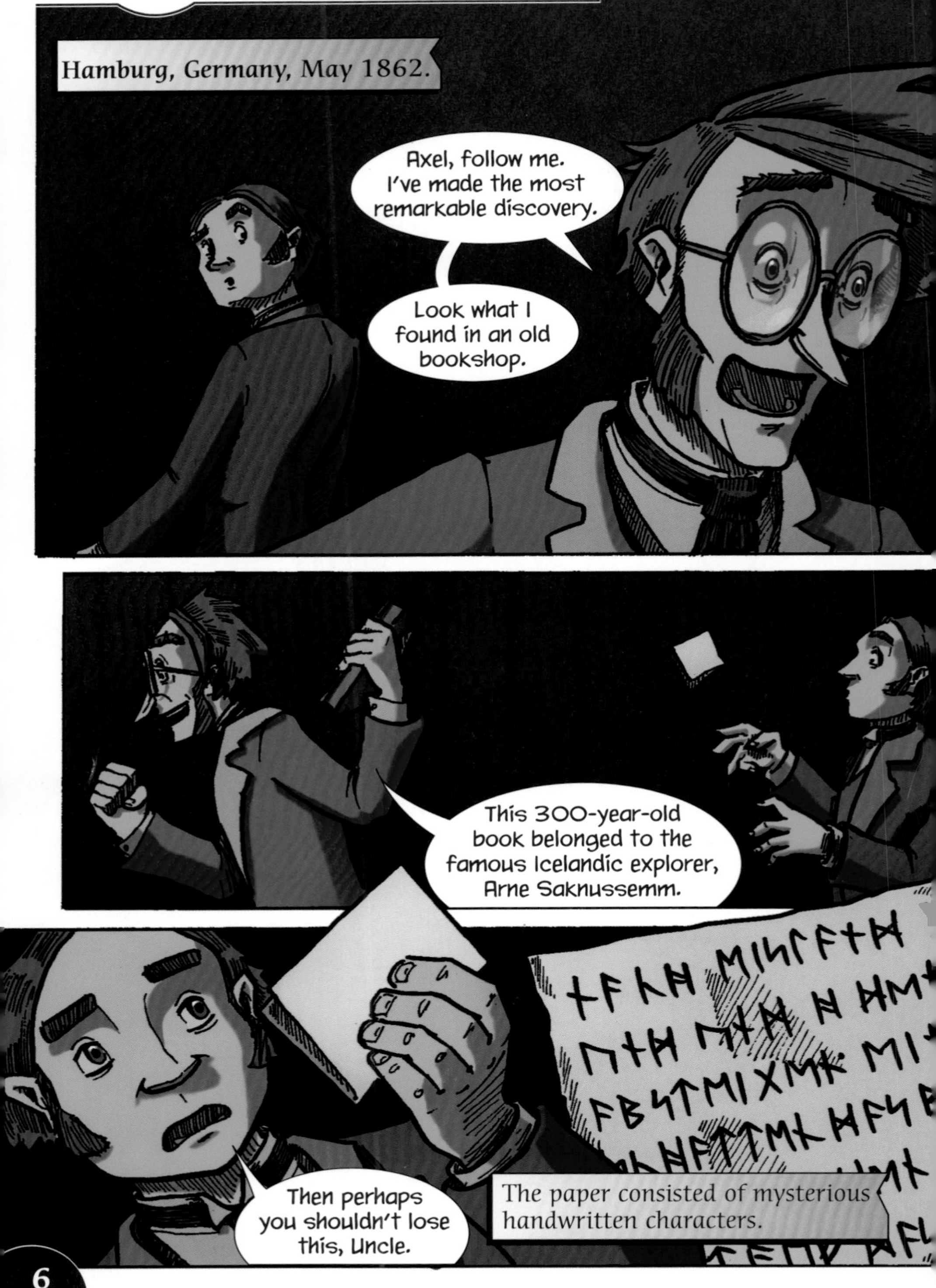
Hamburg, Germany, May 1862.
Axel, follow me. I've made the most remarkable discovery.
Look what I found in an old bookshop.
This 300-year-old book belonged to the famous Icelandic explorer, Arne Saknussemm.
Then perhaps you shouldn't lose this, Uncle.
The paper consisted of mysterious handwritten characters.

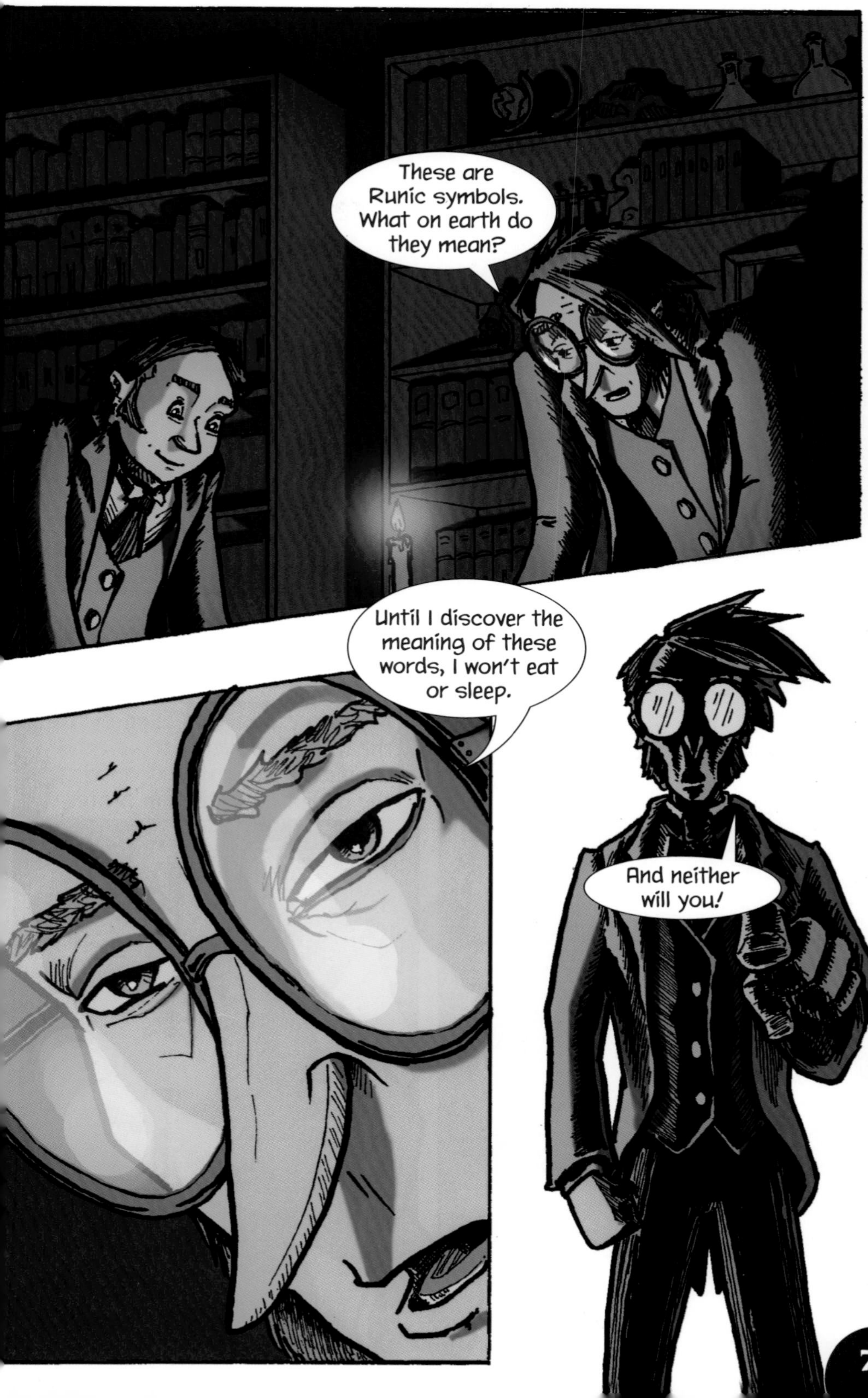
These are Runic symbols. What on earth do they mean?
Until I discover the meaning of these words, I won't eat or sleep.
And neither will you!

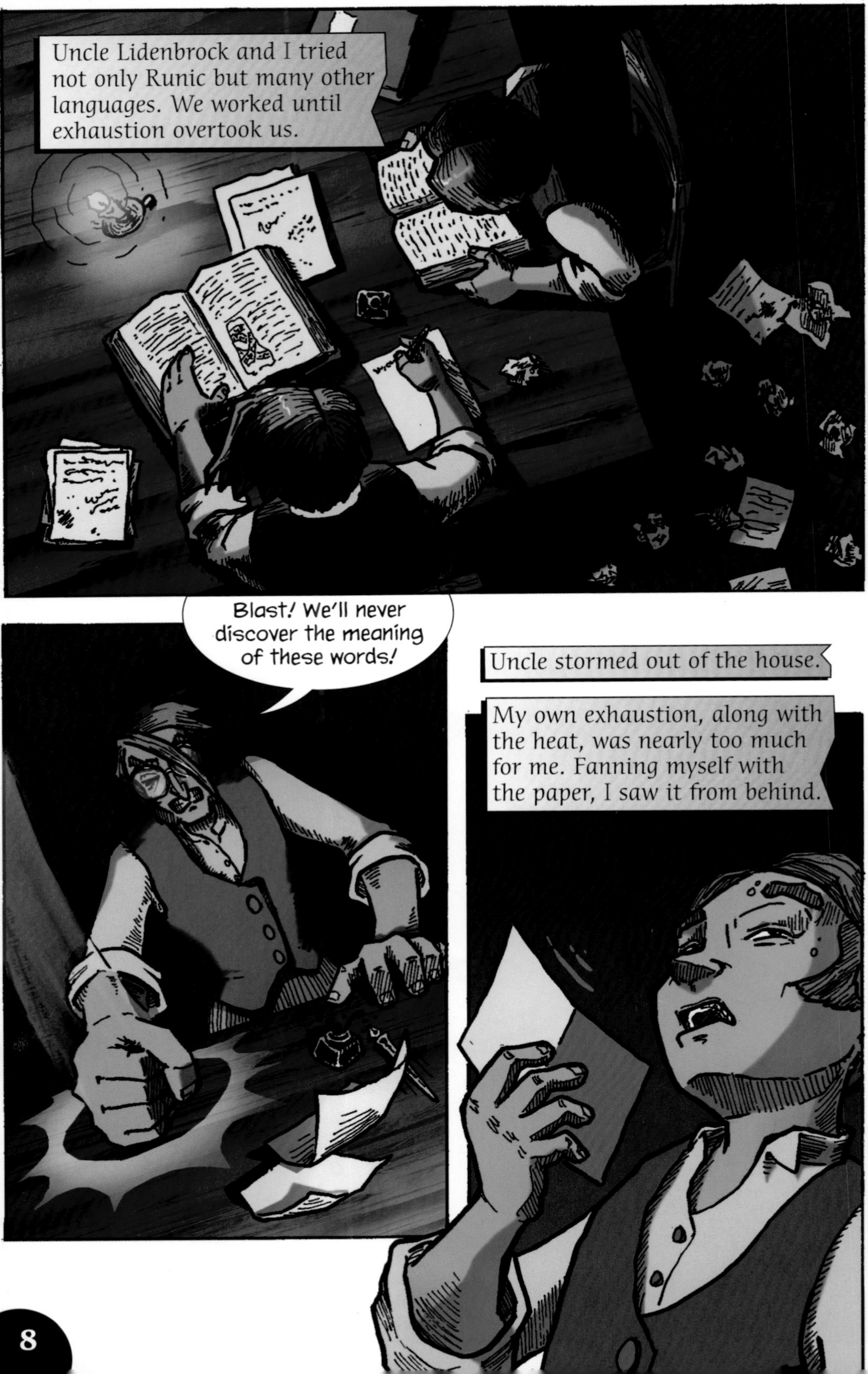
Uncle Lidenbrock and I tried not only Runic but many other languages. We worked until exhaustion overtook us.
Blast! We'll never discover the meaning of these words!
Uncle stormed out of the house.
My own exhaustion, along with the heat, was nearly too much for me. Fanning myself with the paper, I saw it from behind.

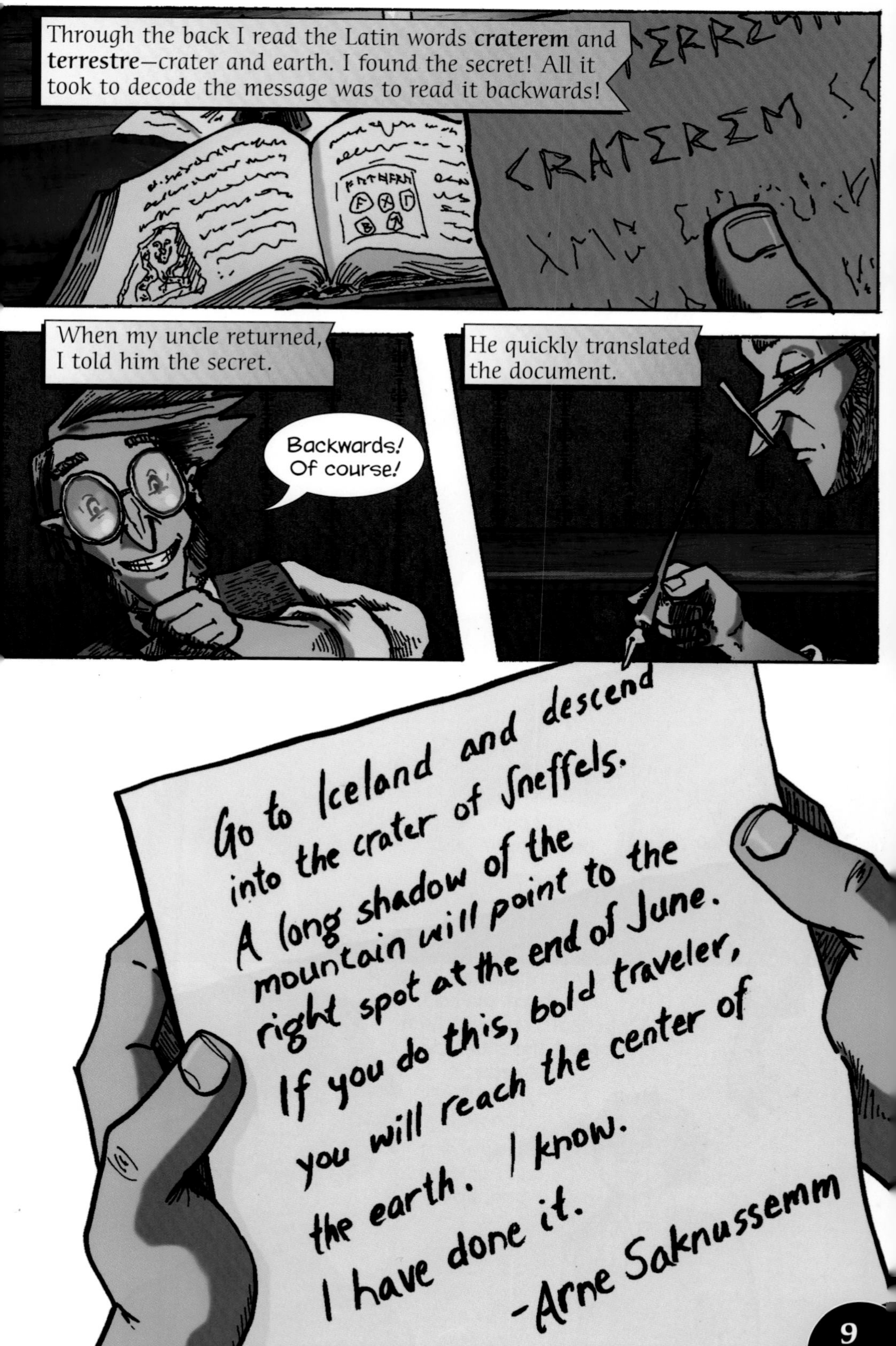
Through the back I read the Latin words **craterem** and **terrestre**—crater and earth. I found the secret! All it took to decode the message was to read it backwards!
CRATEREM
When my uncle returned, I told him the secret.
Backwards! Of course!
He quickly translated the document.
Go to Iceland and descend into the crater of Sneffels. A long shadow of the mountain will point to the right spot at the end of June. If you do this, bold traveler, you will reach the center of the earth. I know. I have done it.
-Arne Saknussemm

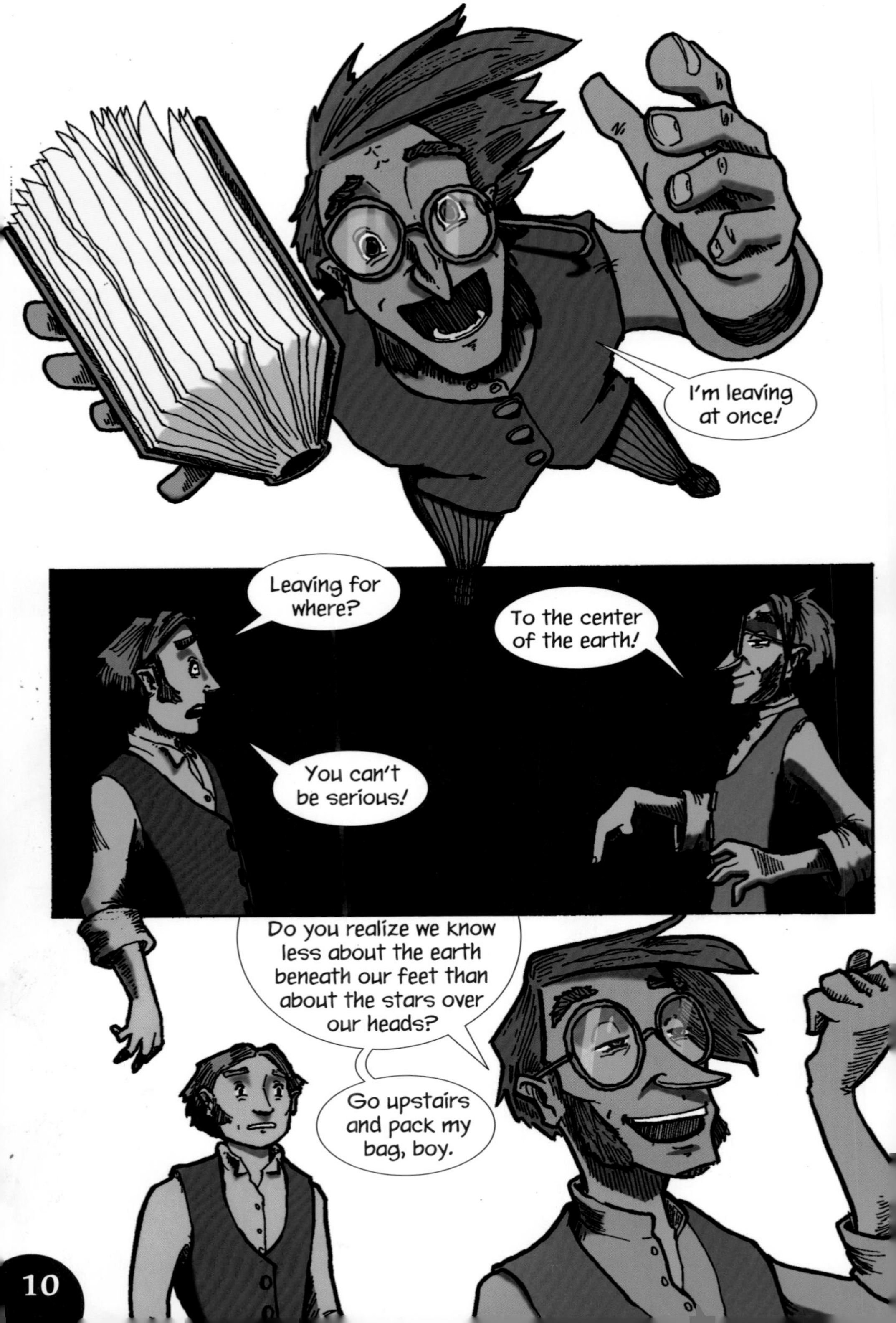
I'm leaving at once!
Leaving for where?
To the center of the earth!
You can't be serious!
Do you realize we know less about the earth beneath our feet than about the stars over our heads?
Go upstairs and pack my bag, boy.

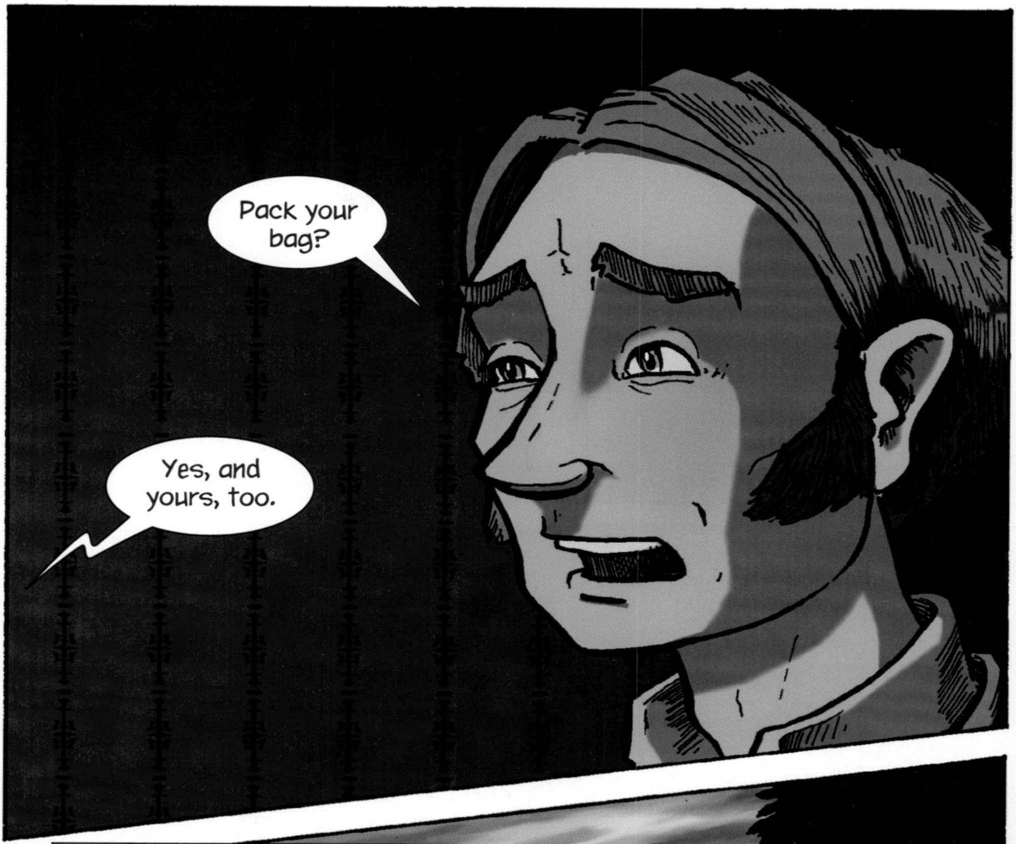
Pack your bag?
Yes, and yours, too.

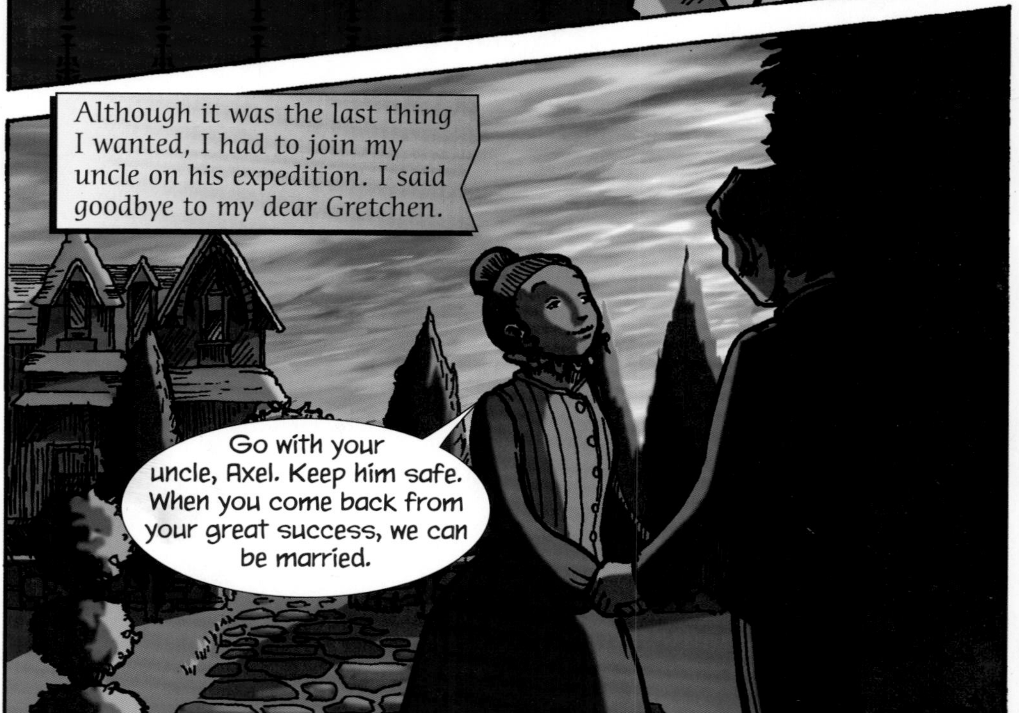
Although it was the last thing I wanted, I had to join my uncle on his expedition. I said goodbye to my dear Gretchen.
Go with your uncle, Axel. Keep him safe. When you come back from your great success, we can be married.

CHAPTER 2 OUR JOURNEY BEGINS

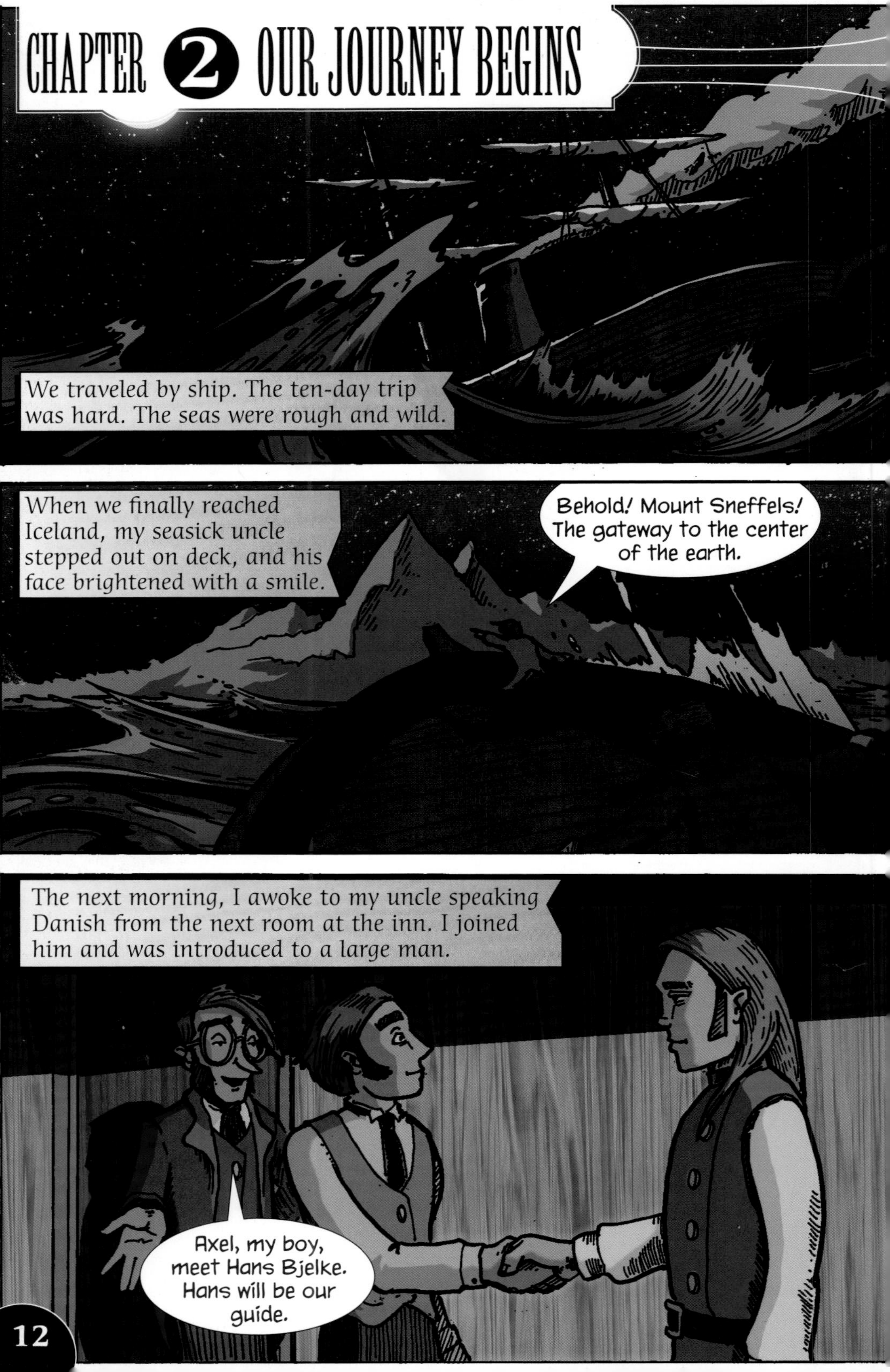

We traveled by ship. The ten-day trip was hard. The seas were rough and wild.
When we finally reached Iceland, my seasick uncle stepped out on deck, and his face brightened with a smile.
Behold! Mount Sneffels! The gateway to the center of the earth.
The next morning, I awoke to my uncle speaking Danish from the next room at the inn. I joined him and was introduced to a large man.
Axel, my boy, meet Hans Bjelke. Hans will be our guide.

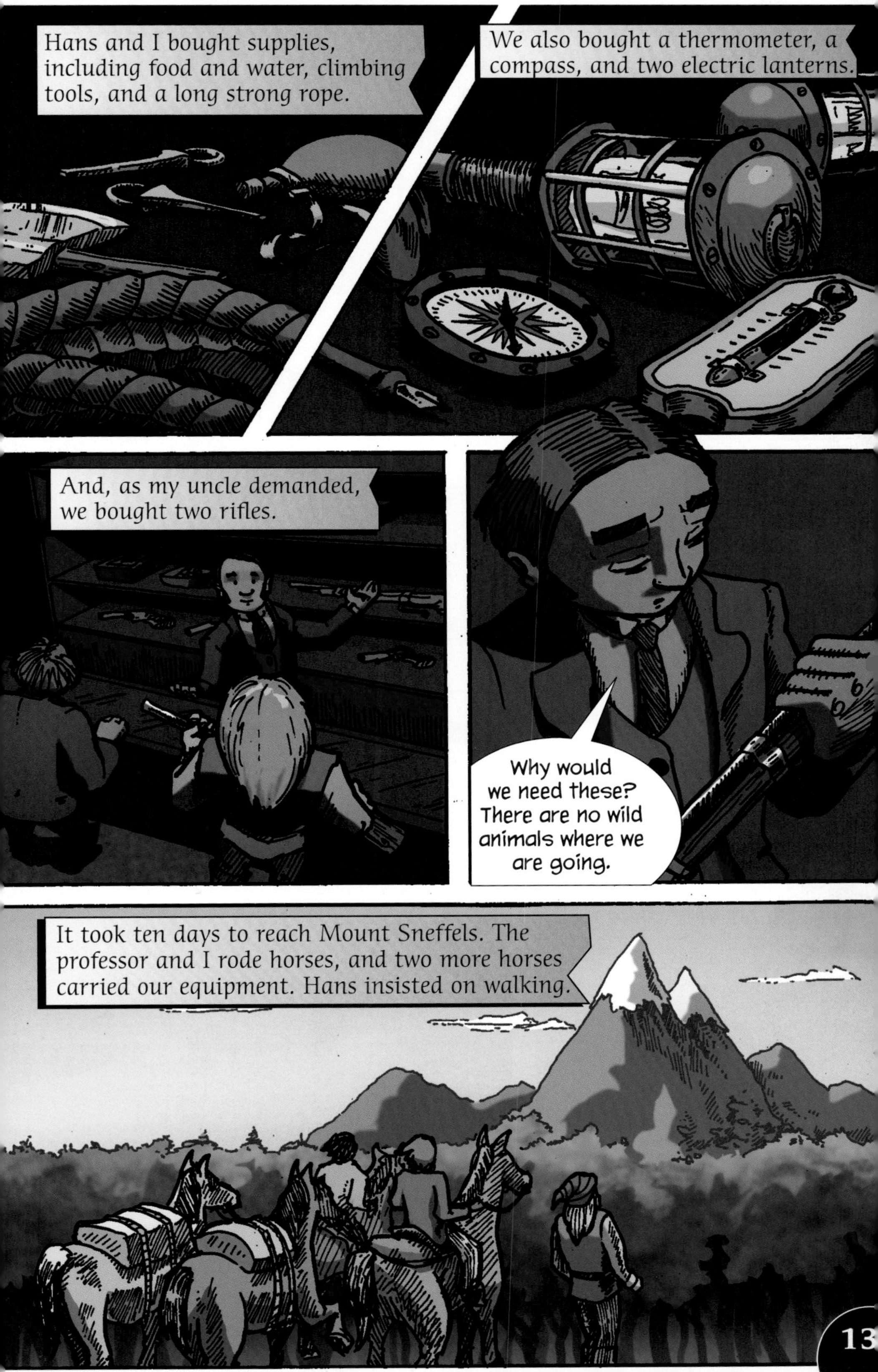
Hans and I bought supplies, including food and water, climbing tools, and a long strong rope.
We also bought a thermometer, a compass, and two electric lanterns.
And, as my uncle demanded, we bought two rifles.
Why would we need these? There are no wild animals where we are going.
It took ten days to reach Mount Sneffels. The professor and I rode horses, and two more horses carried our equipment. Hans insisted on walking.

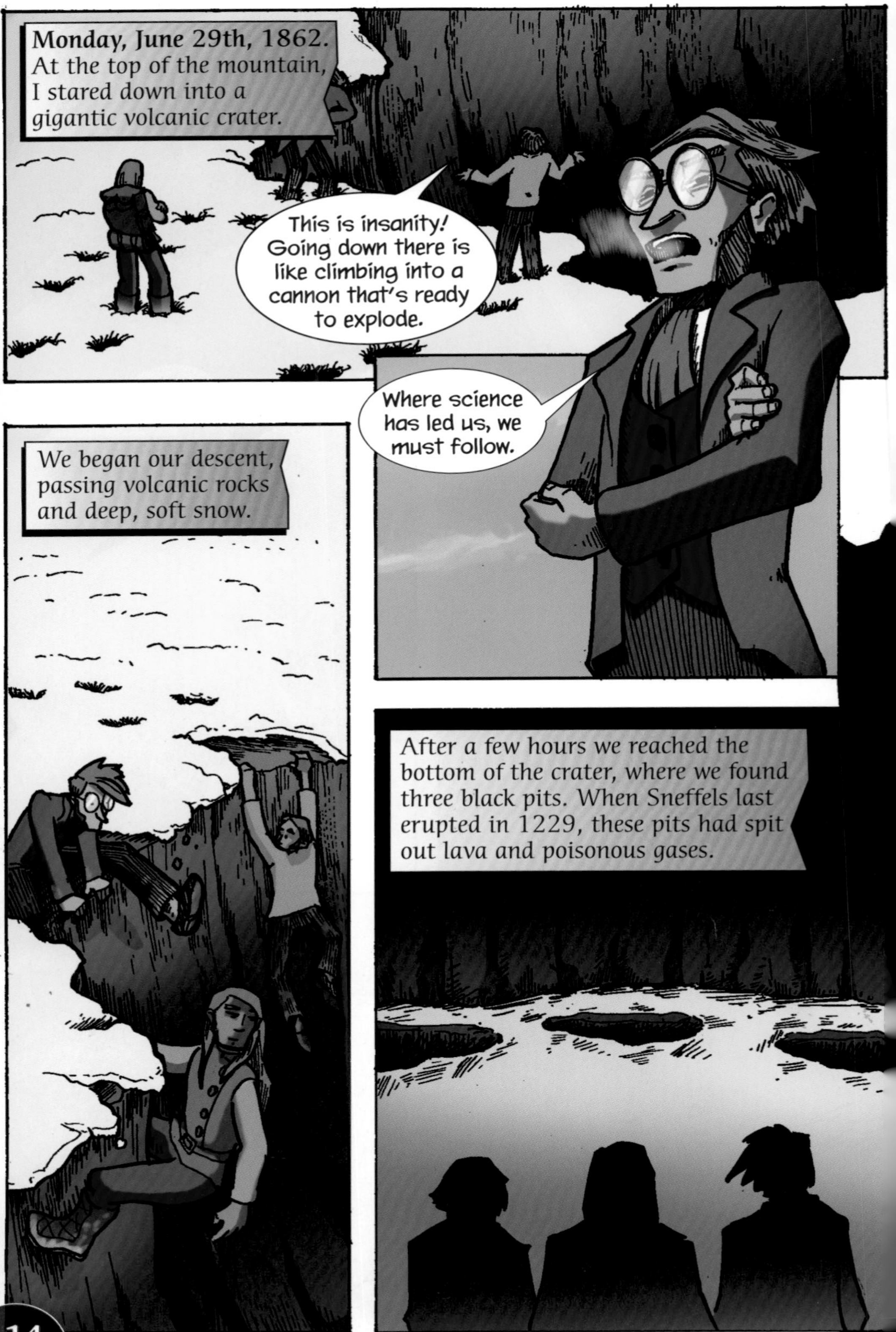
Monday, June 29th, 1862. At the top of the mountain, I stared down into a gigantic volcanic crater.
This is insanity! Going down there is like climbing into a cannon that's ready to explode.
Where science has led us, we must follow.
We began our descent, passing volcanic rocks and deep, soft snow.
After a few hours we reached the bottom of the crater, where we found three black pits. When Sneffels last erupted in 1229, these pits had spit out lava and poisonous gases.

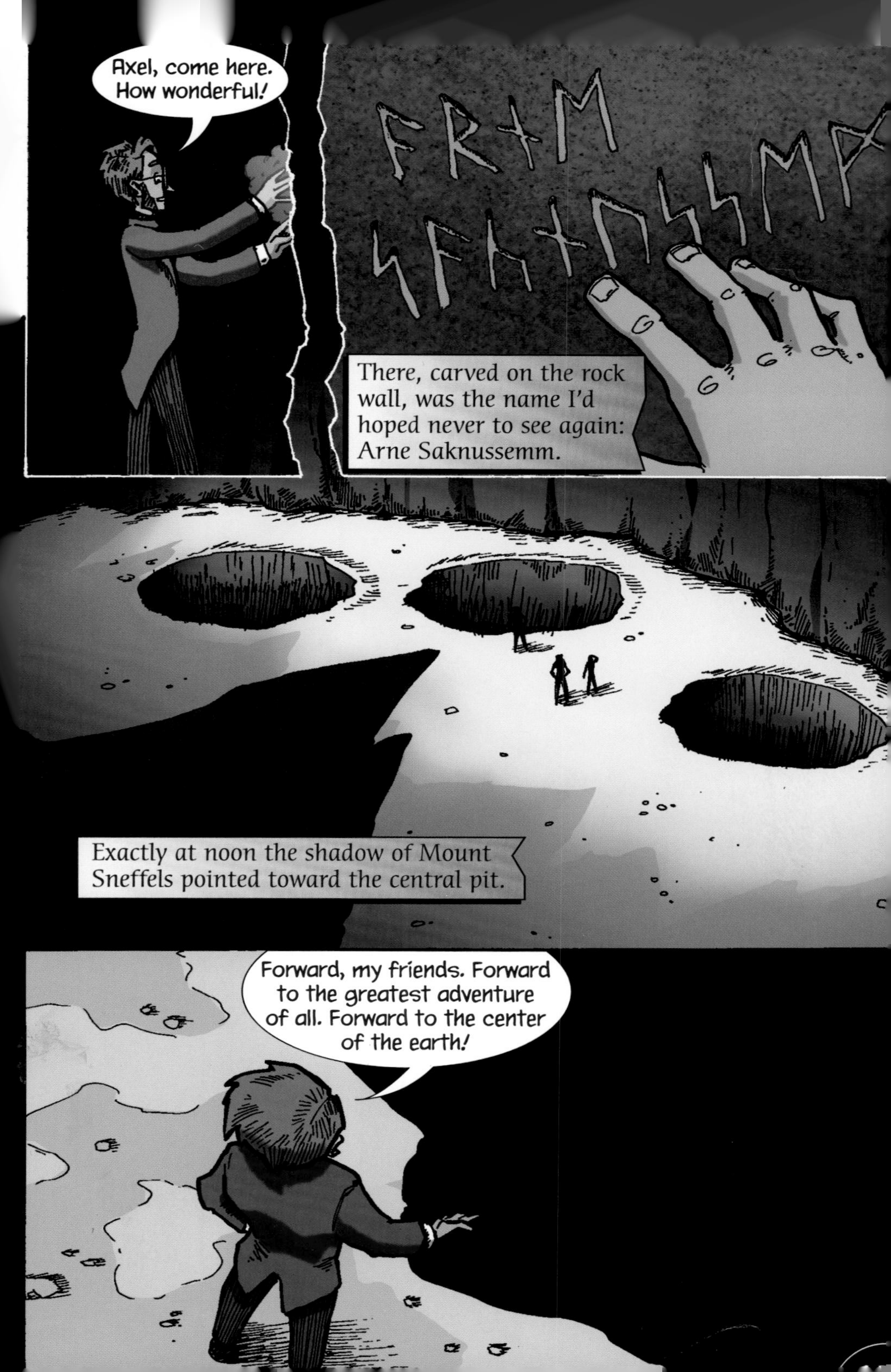
Axel, come here. How wonderful!
There, carved on the rock wall, was the name I'd hoped never to see again: Arne Saknussemm.
Exactly at noon the shadow of Mount Sneffels pointed toward the central pit.
Forward, my friends. Forward to the greatest adventure of all. Forward to the center of the earth!

The next day, our real journey began. We stepped to the mouth of the central pit. The sides dropped straight down and ended in nothingness. I became dizzy.

My legs went weak.

If not for Hans, I would have fallen to my death.

With a rope tied around a block of hardened lava, we began our descent.

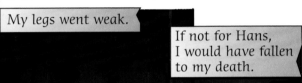

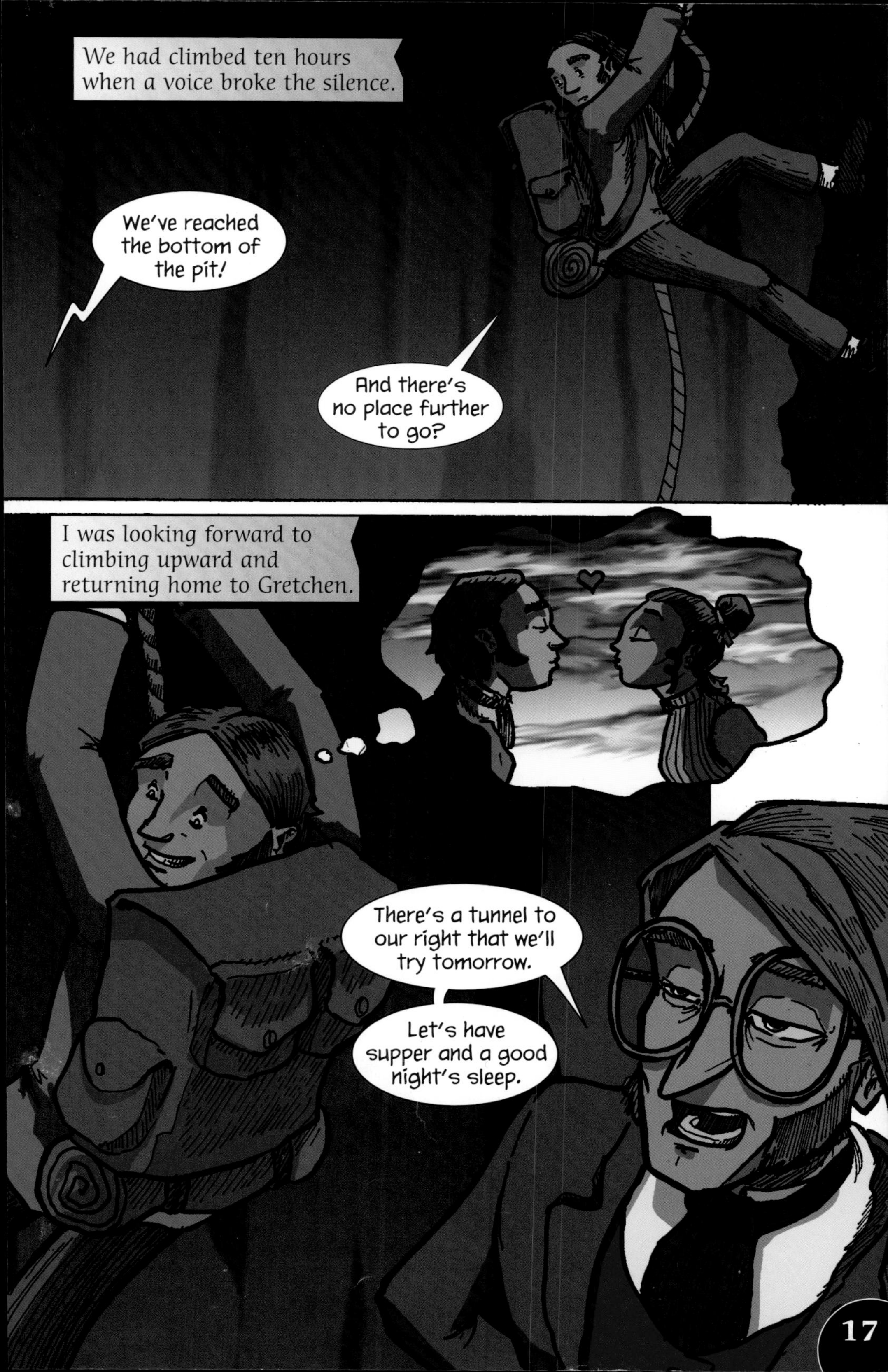

We had climbed ten hours when a voice broke the silence.
We've reached the bottom of the pit!
And there's no place further to go?
I was looking forward to climbing upward and returning home to Gretchen.
There's a tunnel to our right that we'll try tomorrow.
Let's have supper and a good night's sleep.

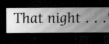

Less than 48 hours into our expedition and we only have enough water for five more days. Doesn't this concern you, Uncle?

No reason to worry. We'll find plenty of water along the way.

On Wednesday, July 1, at six o'clock in the morning, we continued on.

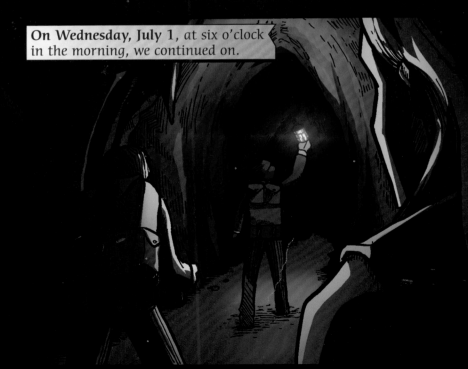

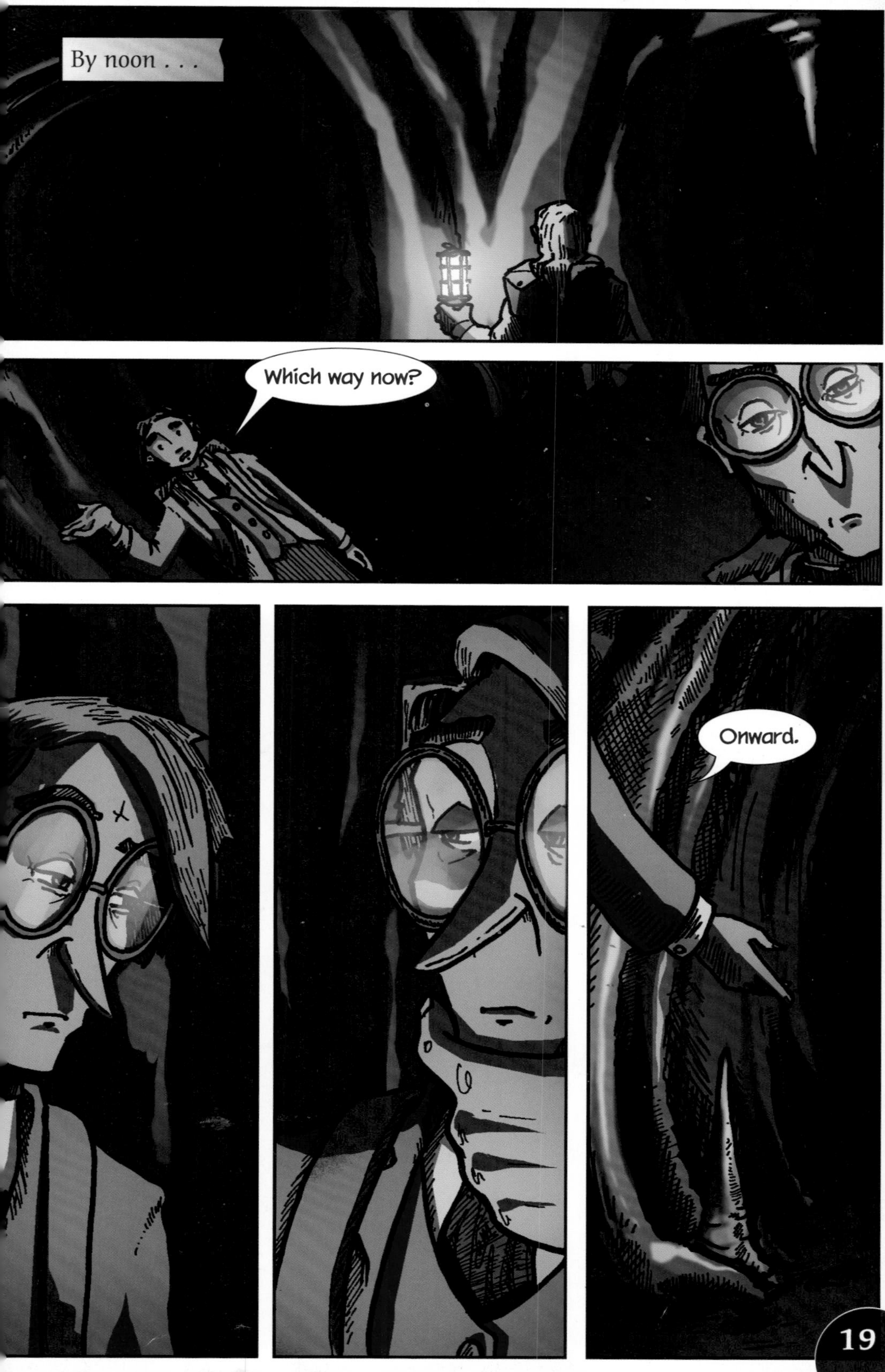
By noon . . .
Which way now?
Onward.

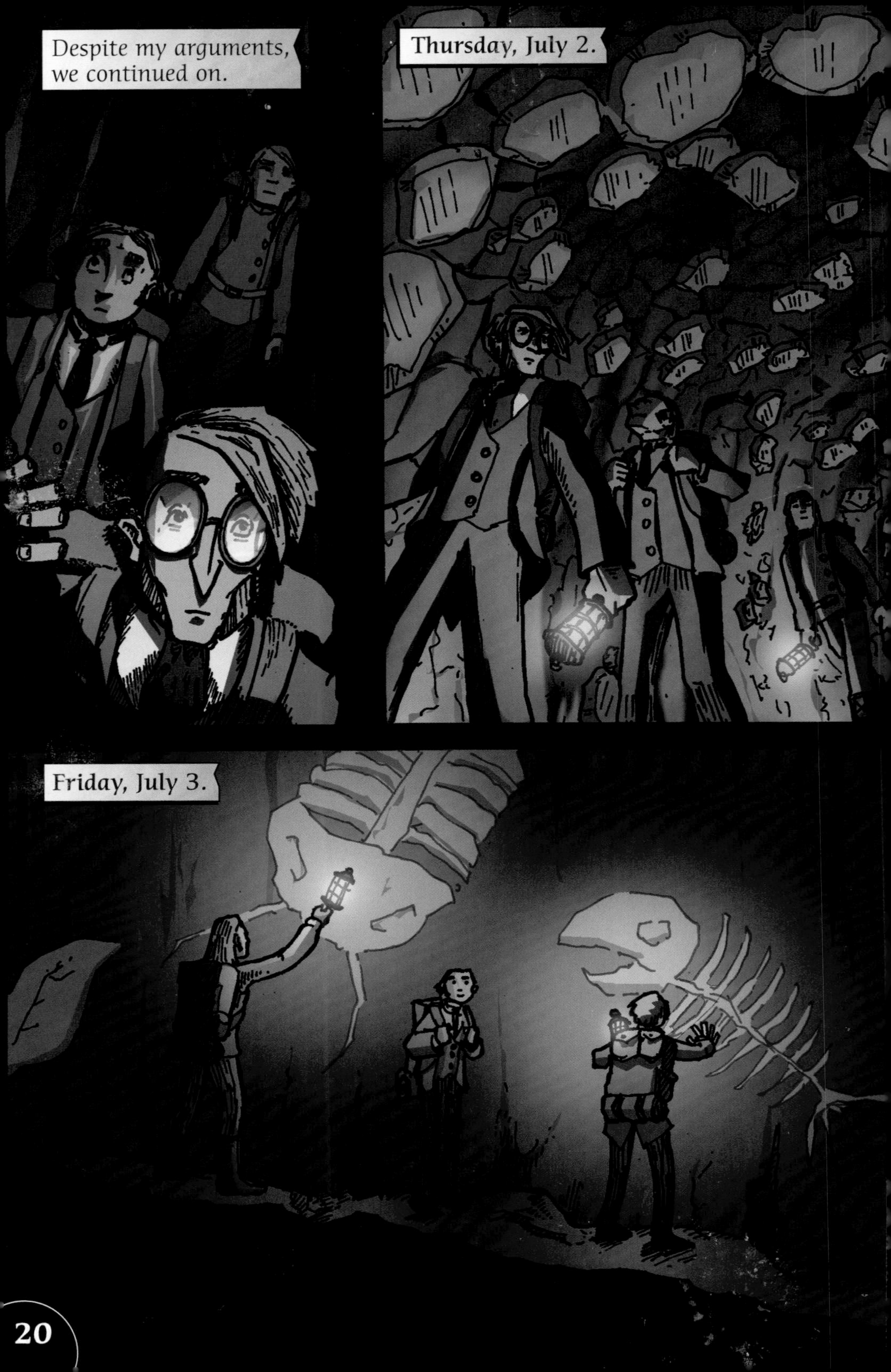
Despite my arguments, we continued on.
Thursday, July 2.
Friday, July 3.

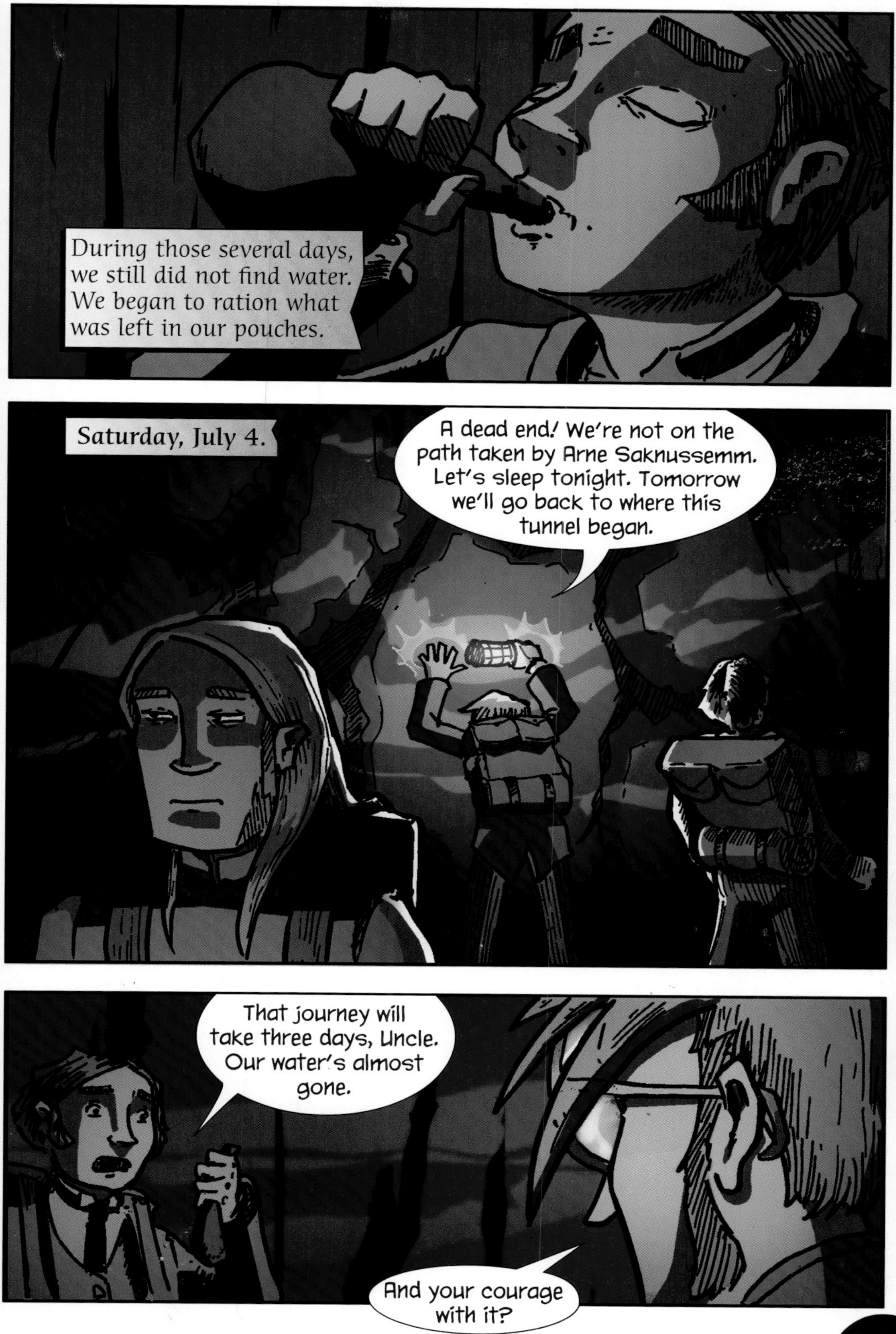
During those several days, we still did not find water. We began to ration what was left in our pouches.
Saturday, July 4.
A dead end! We're not on the path taken by Arne Saknussemm. Let's sleep tonight. Tomorrow we'll go back to where this tunnel began.
That journey will take three days, Uncle. Our water's almost gone.
And your courage with it?

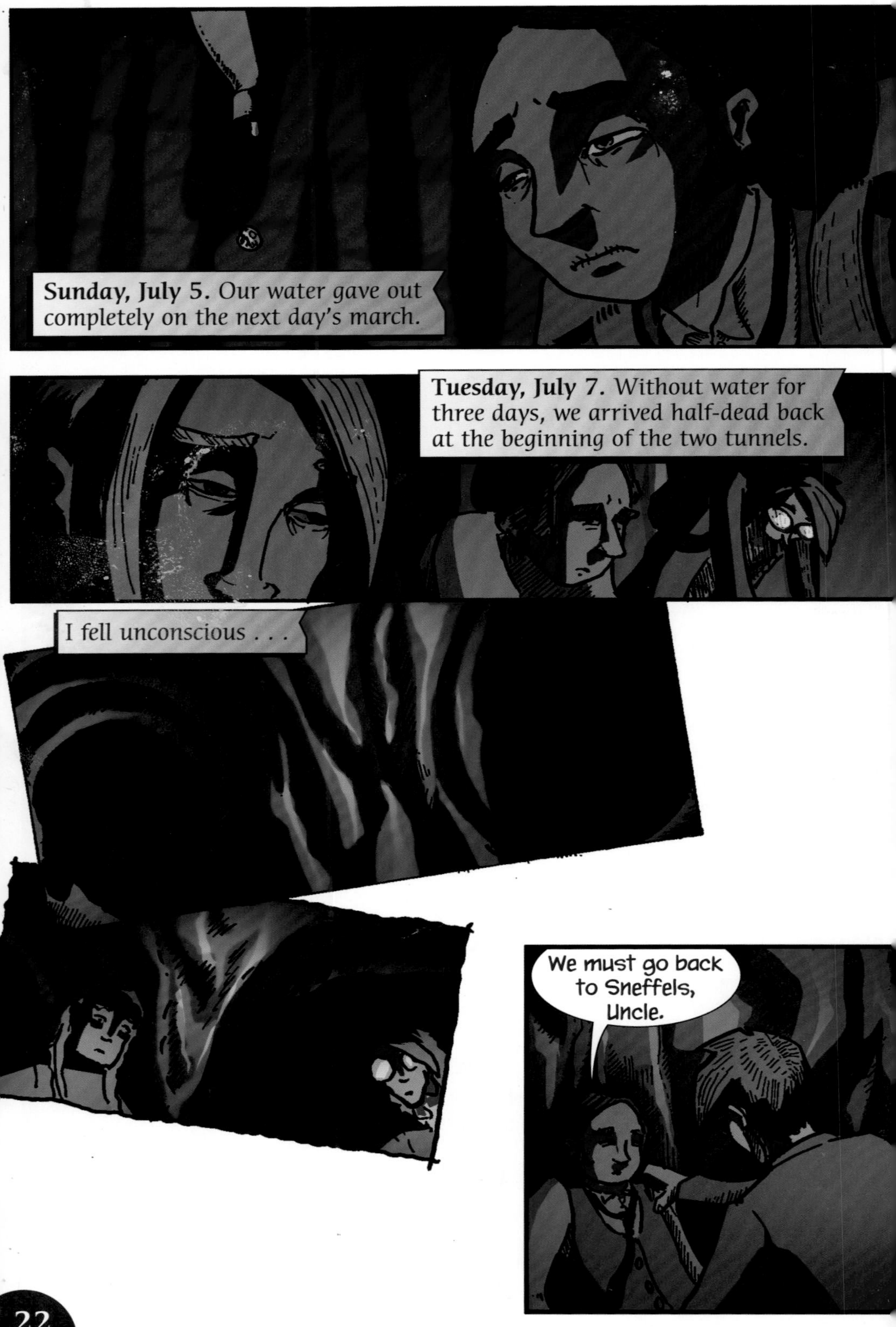
Sunday, July 5. Our water gave out completely on the next day's march.
Tuesday, July 7. Without water for three days, we arrived half-dead back at the beginning of the two tunnels.
I fell unconscious . . .
We must go back to Sneffels, Uncle.

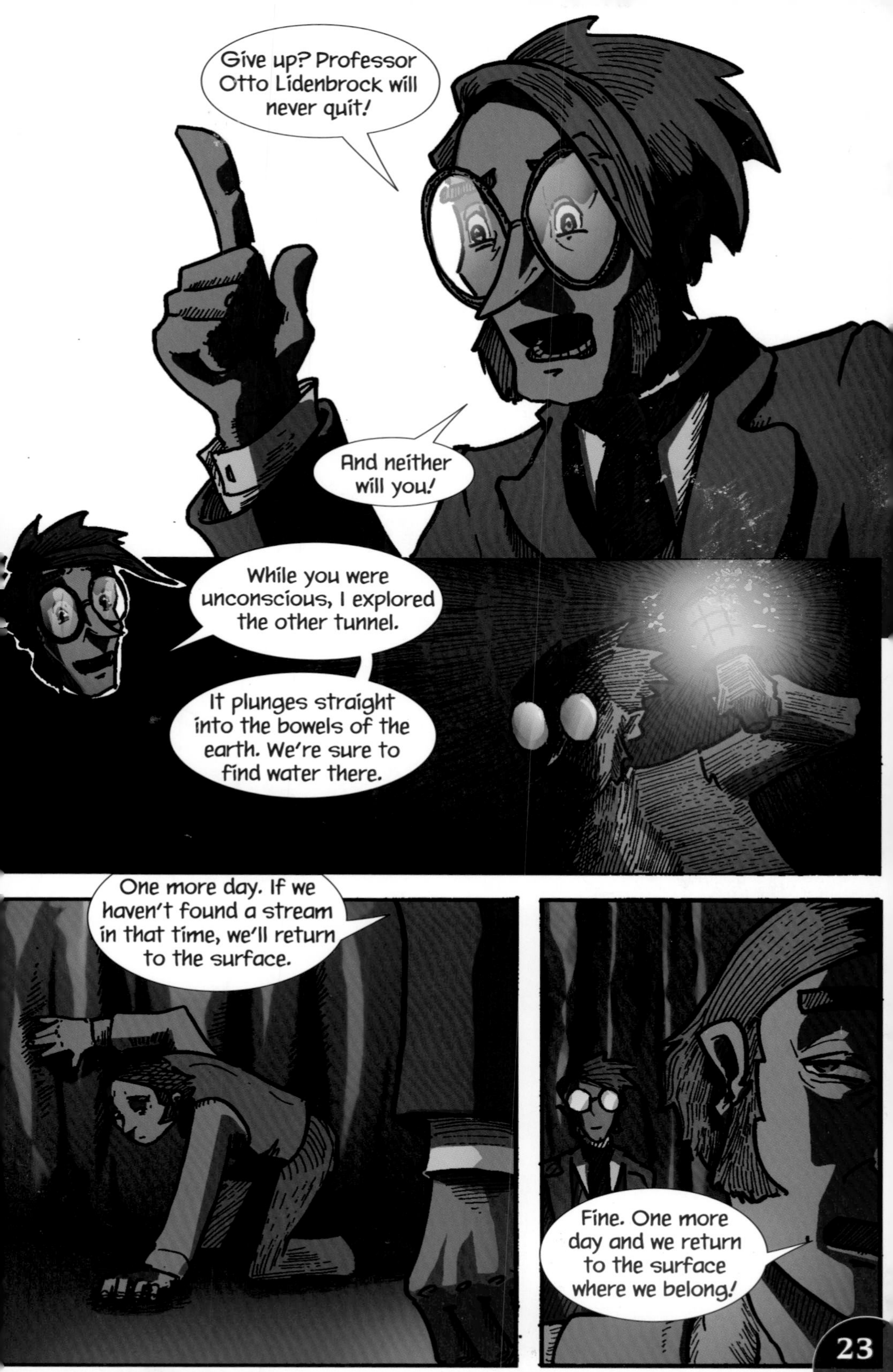
Give up? Professor Otto Lidenbrock will never quit!
And neither will you!
While you were unconscious, I explored the other tunnel.
It plunges straight into the bowels of the earth. We're sure to find water there.
One more day. If we haven't found a stream in that time, we'll return to the surface.
Fine. One more day and we return to the surface where we belong!

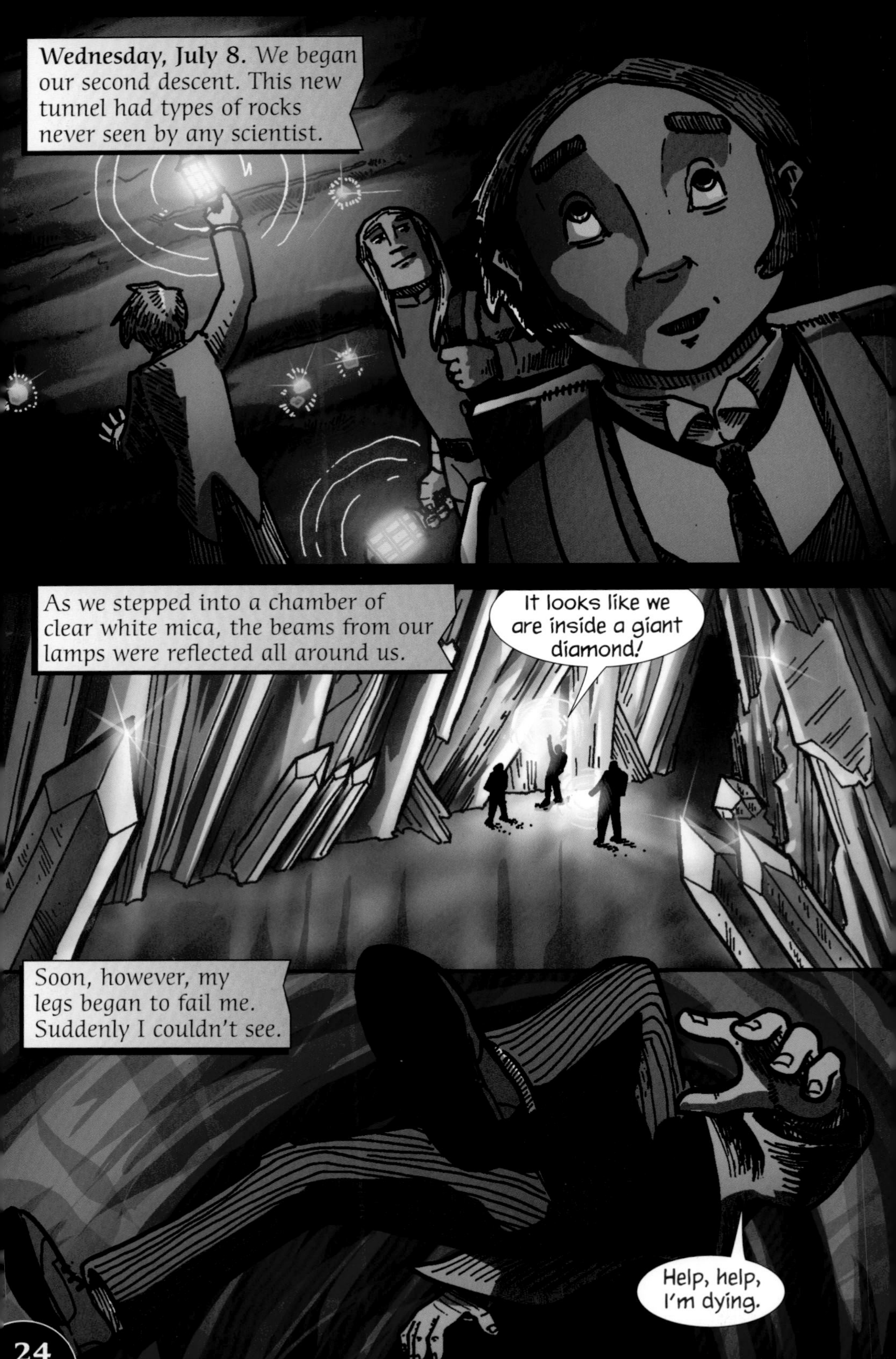
Wednesday, July 8. We began our second descent. This new tunnel had types of rocks never seen by any scientist.
As we stepped into a chamber of clear white mica, the beams from our lamps were reflected all around us.
It looks like we are inside a giant diamond!
Soon, however, my legs began to fail me. Suddenly I couldn't see.
Help, help, I'm dying.

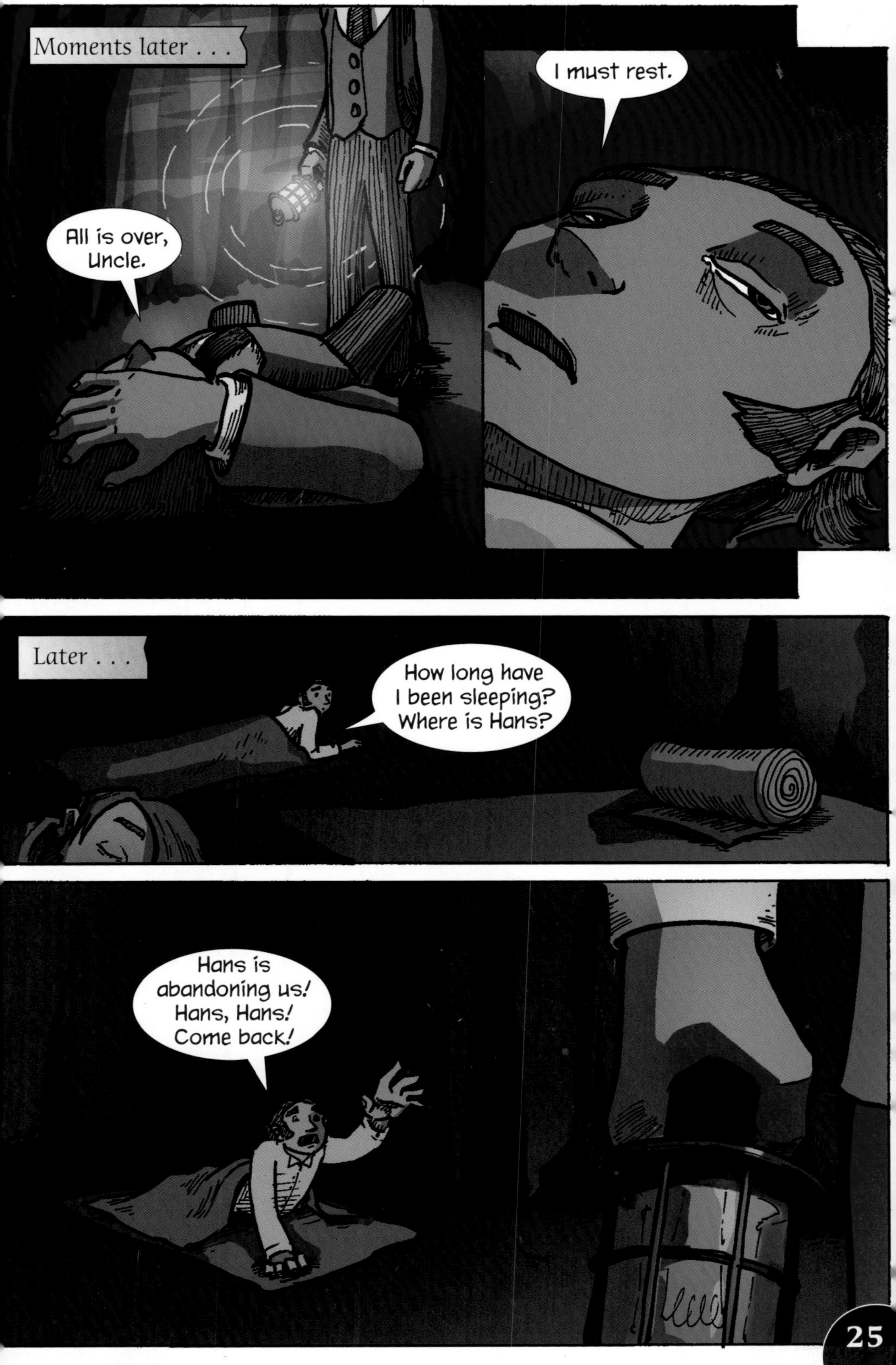
Moments later . . .
All is over, Uncle.
I must rest.
Later . . .
How long have I been sleeping? Where is Hans?
Hans is abandoning us! Hans, Hans! Come back!

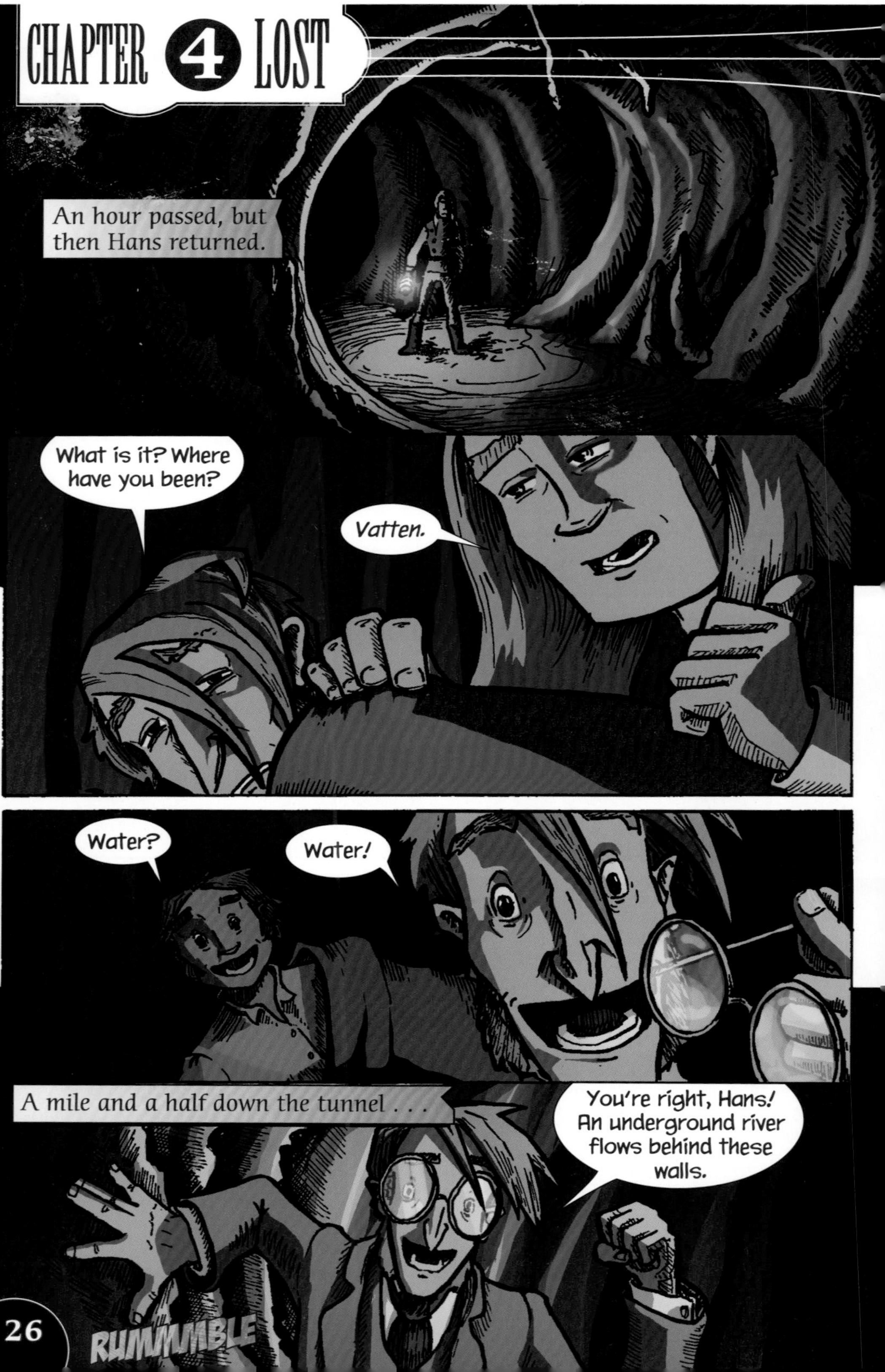
CHAPTER 4 LOST
An hour passed, but then Hans returned.
What is it? Where have you been?
Vatten.
Water?
Water!
A mile and a half down the tunnel . . .
You're right, Hans! An underground river flows behind these walls.
RUMMMBLE

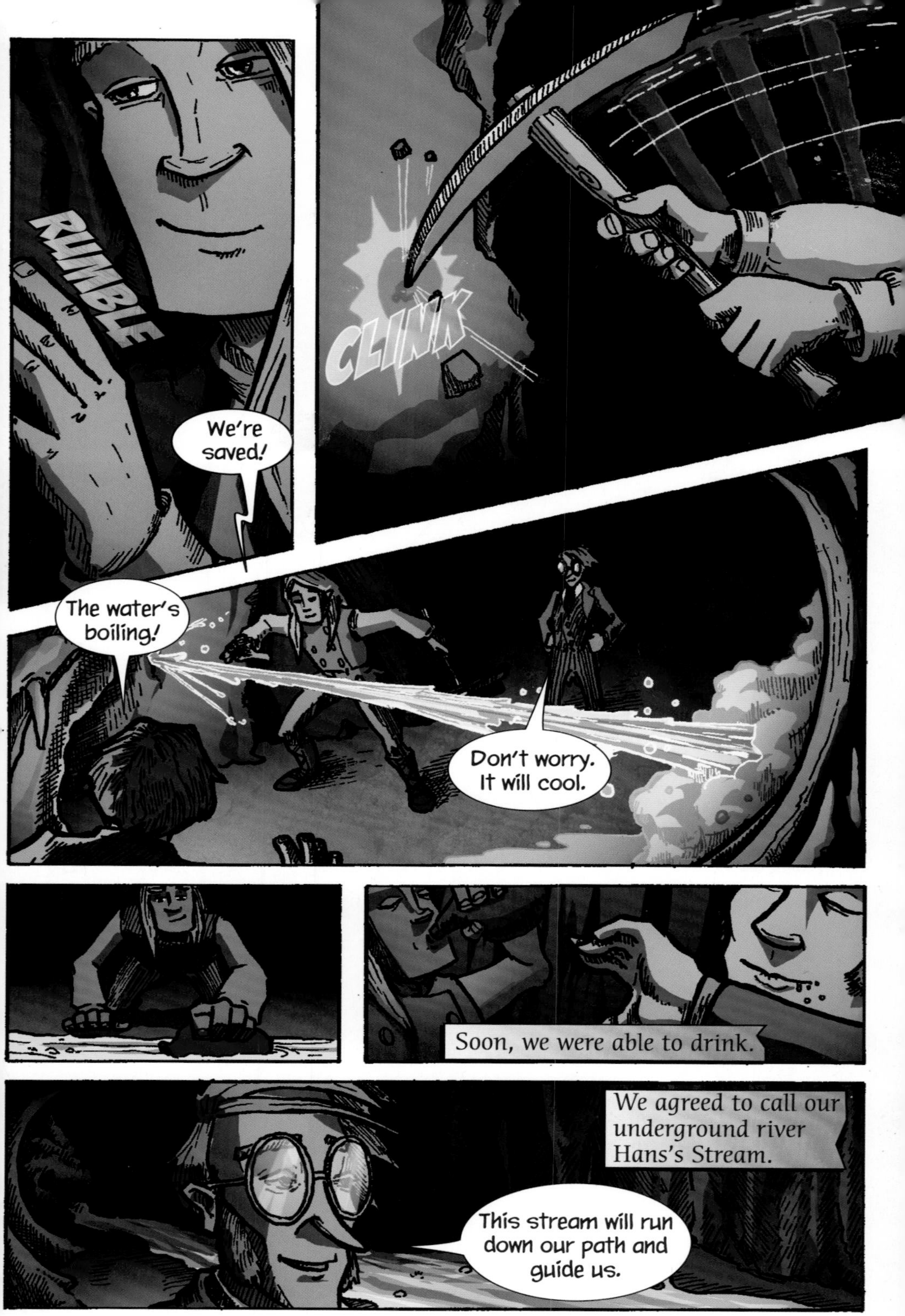
RUMBLE
We're saved!
CLINK
The water's boiling!
Don't worry. It will cool.
Soon, we were able to drink.
We agreed to call our underground river Hans's Stream.
This stream will run down our path and guide us.

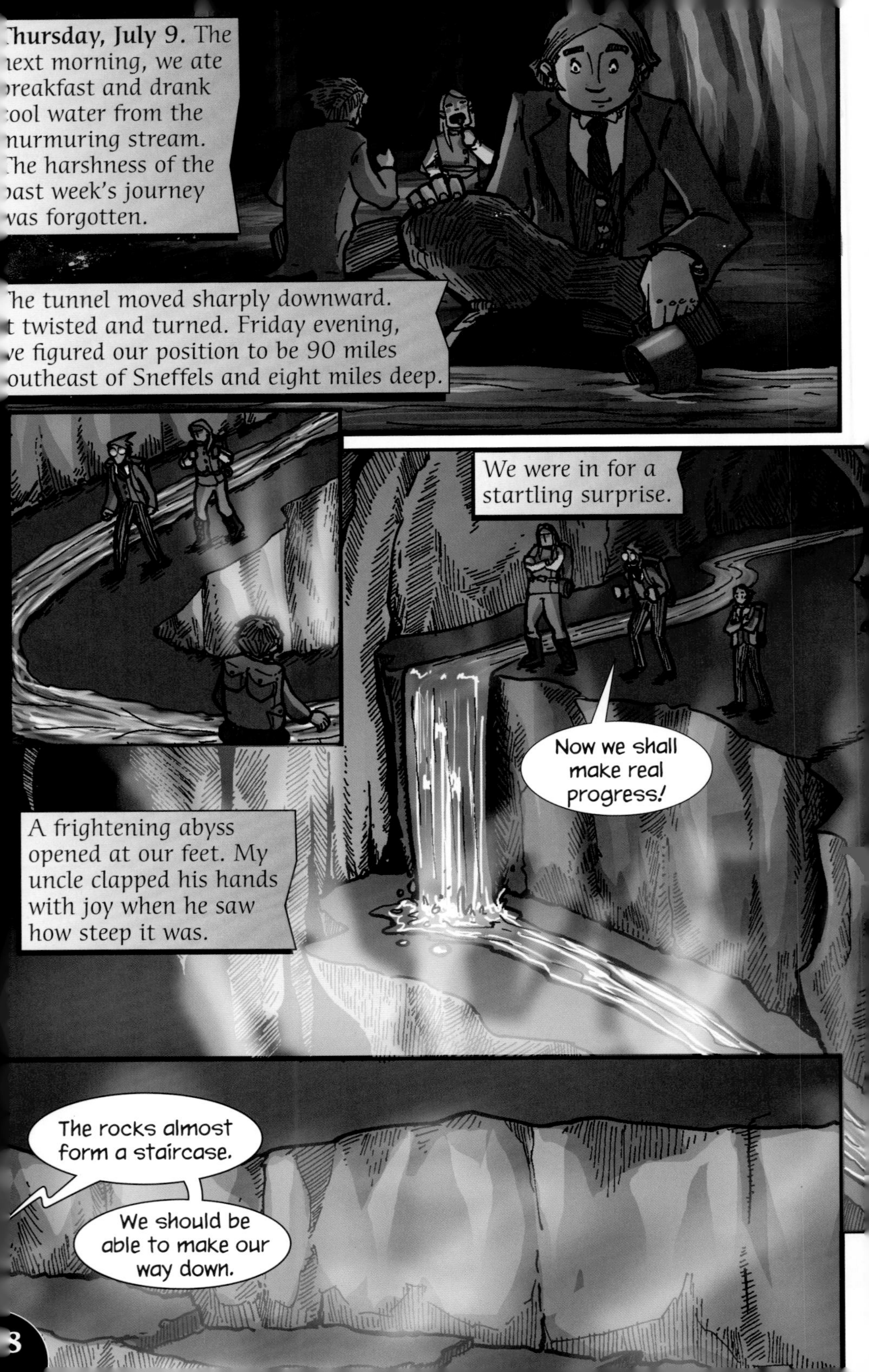
Thursday, July 9. The next morning, we ate breakfast and drank cool water from the murmuring stream. The harshness of the past week's journey was forgotten.
The tunnel moved sharply downward. It twisted and turned. Friday evening, we figured our position to be 90 miles southeast of Sneffels and eight miles deep.
We were in for a startling surprise.
Now we shall make real progress!
A frightening abyss opened at our feet. My uncle clapped his hands with joy when he saw how steep it was.
The rocks almost form a staircase.
We should be able to make our way down.

We followed the staircase deeper and deeper into the earth, the loyal stream flowing beside us.

Our spiral road carried us 20 miles below sea level.

Our toil took us deeper into the earth. Above our heads: rocks, ocean, a continent, entire cities of people.

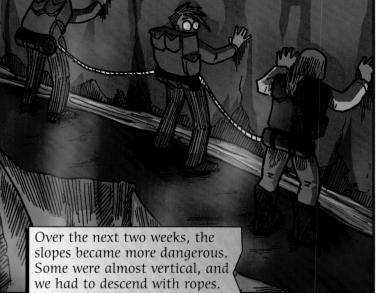

Over the next two weeks, the slopes became more dangerous. Some were almost vertical, and we had to descend with ropes.

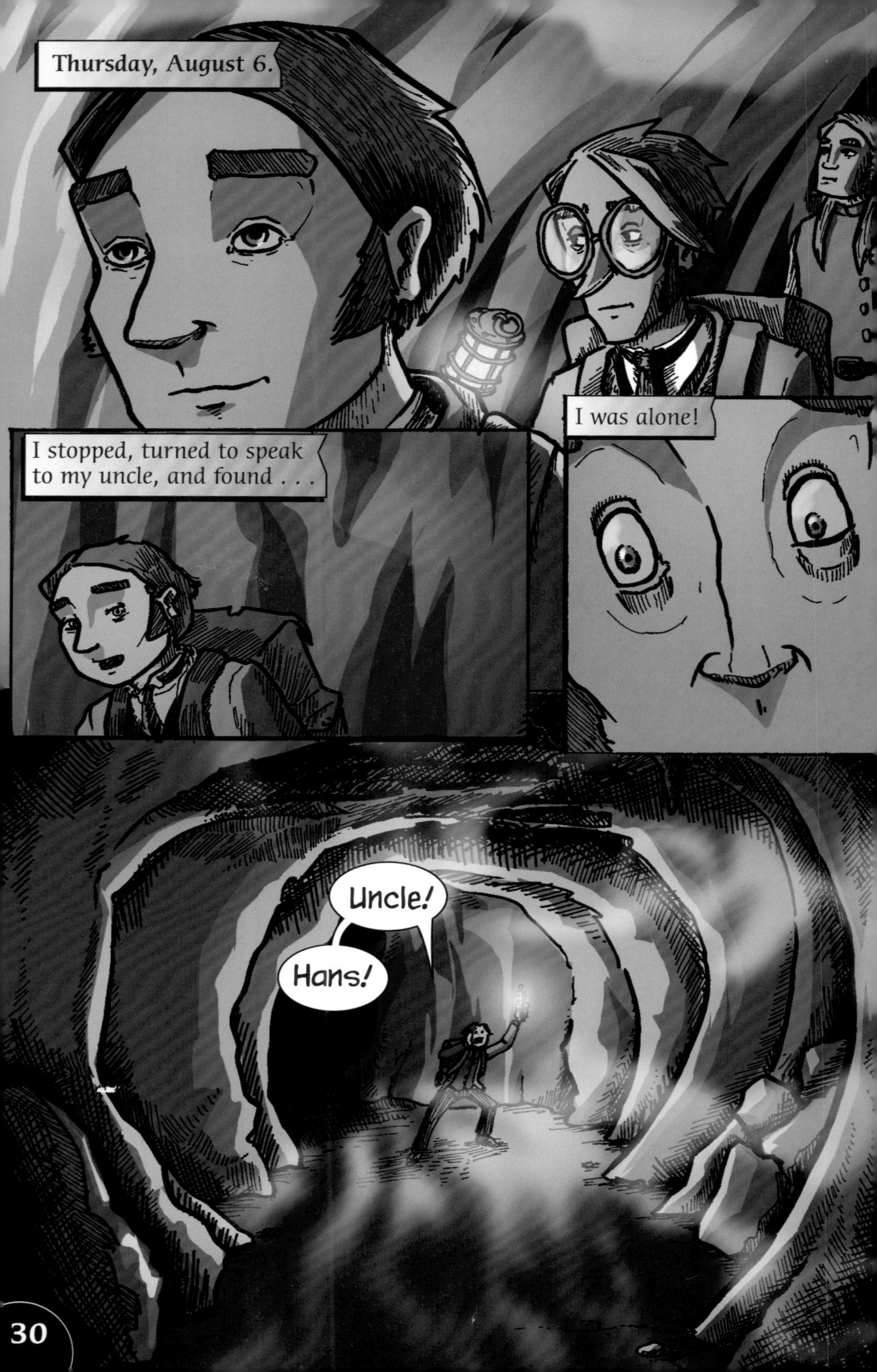
Thursday, August 6.
I stopped, turned to speak to my uncle, and found . . .
I was alone!
Uncle!
Hans!

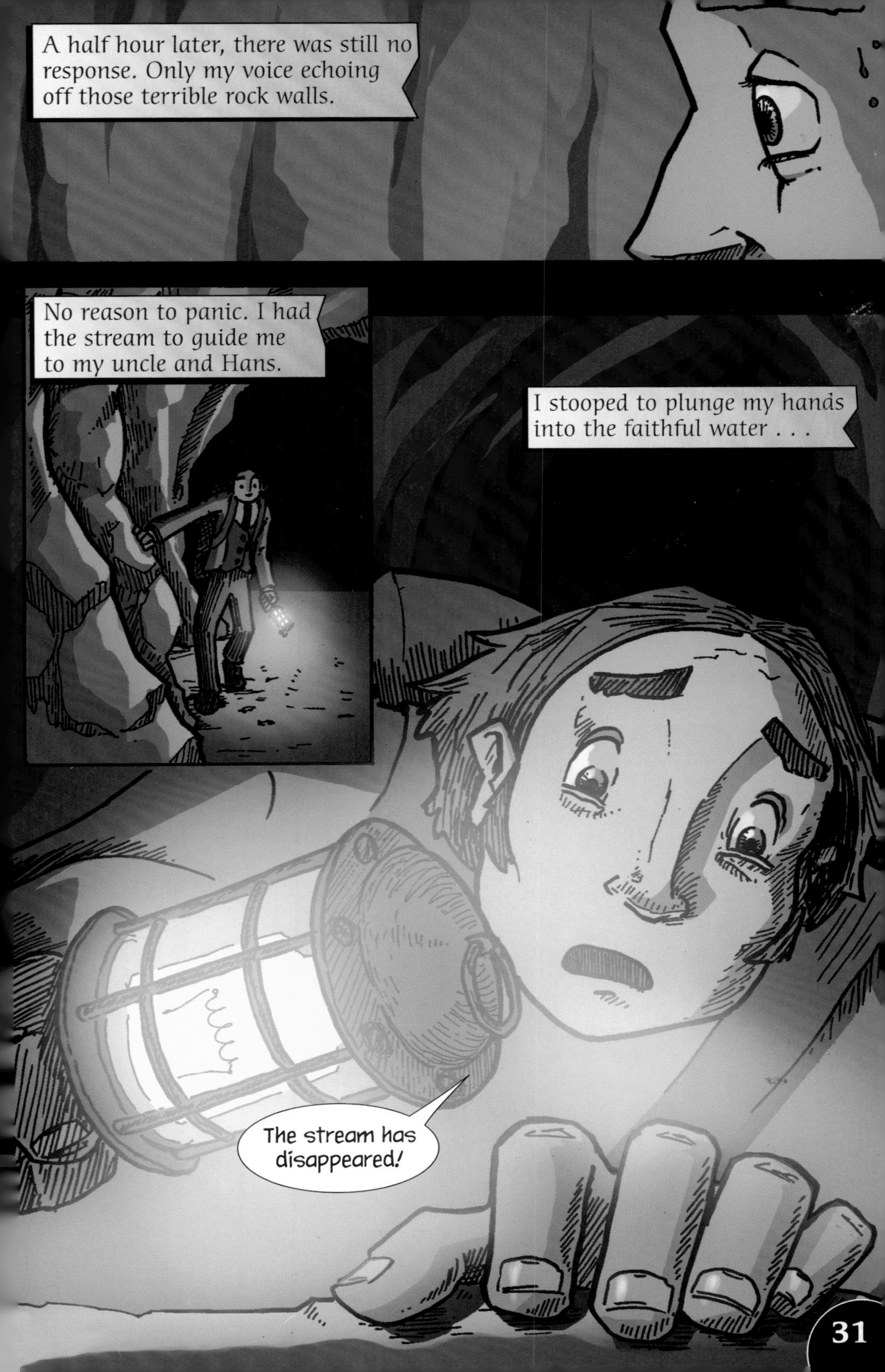
A half hour later, there was still no response. Only my voice echoing off those terrible rock walls.
No reason to panic. I had the stream to guide me to my uncle and Hans.
I stooped to plunge my hands into the faithful water . . .
The stream has disappeared!

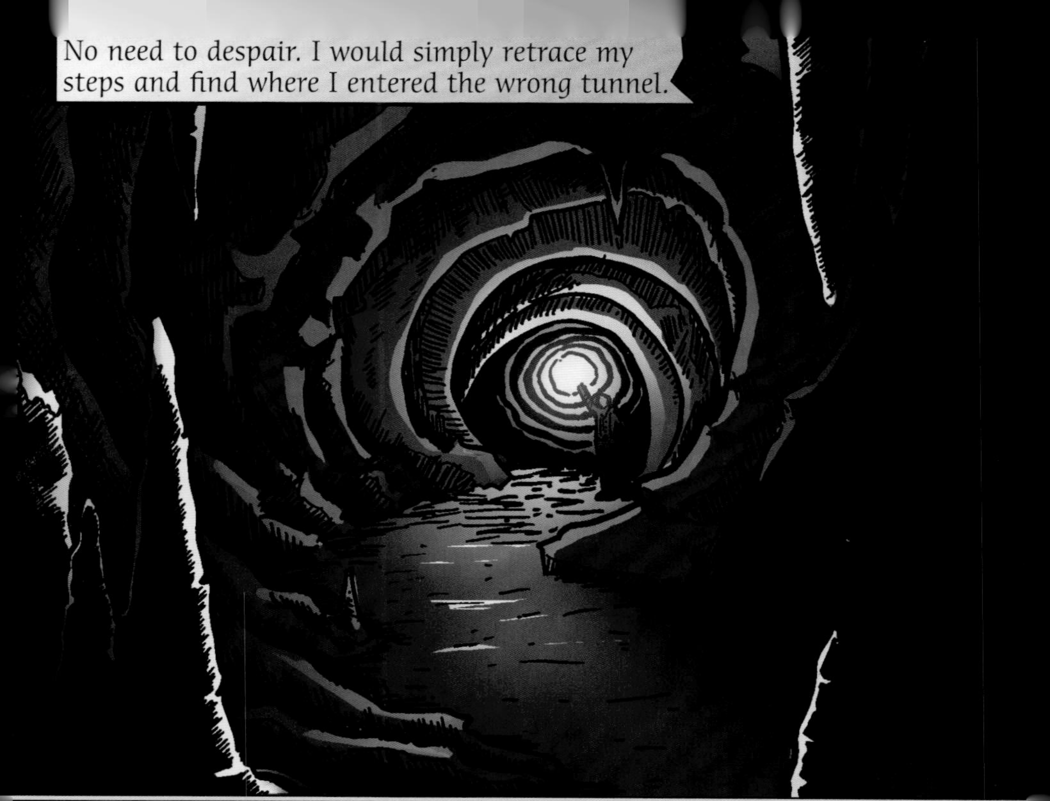
No need to despair. I would simply retrace my steps and find where I entered the wrong tunnel.

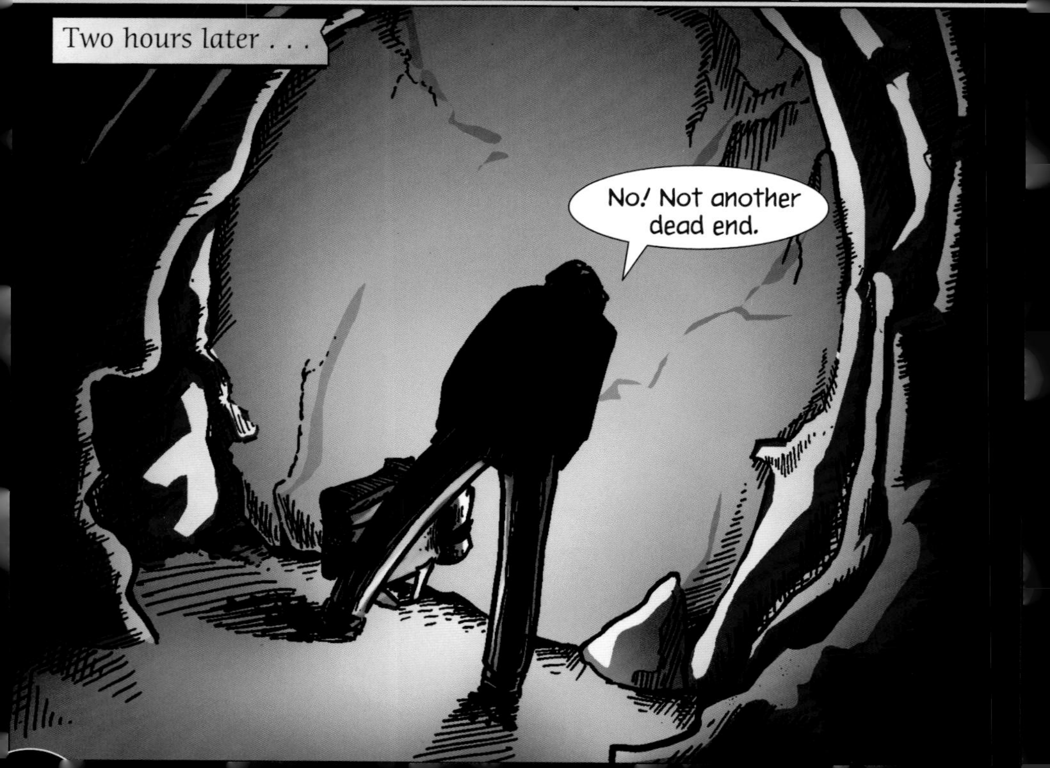
Two hours later . . .
No! Not another dead end.

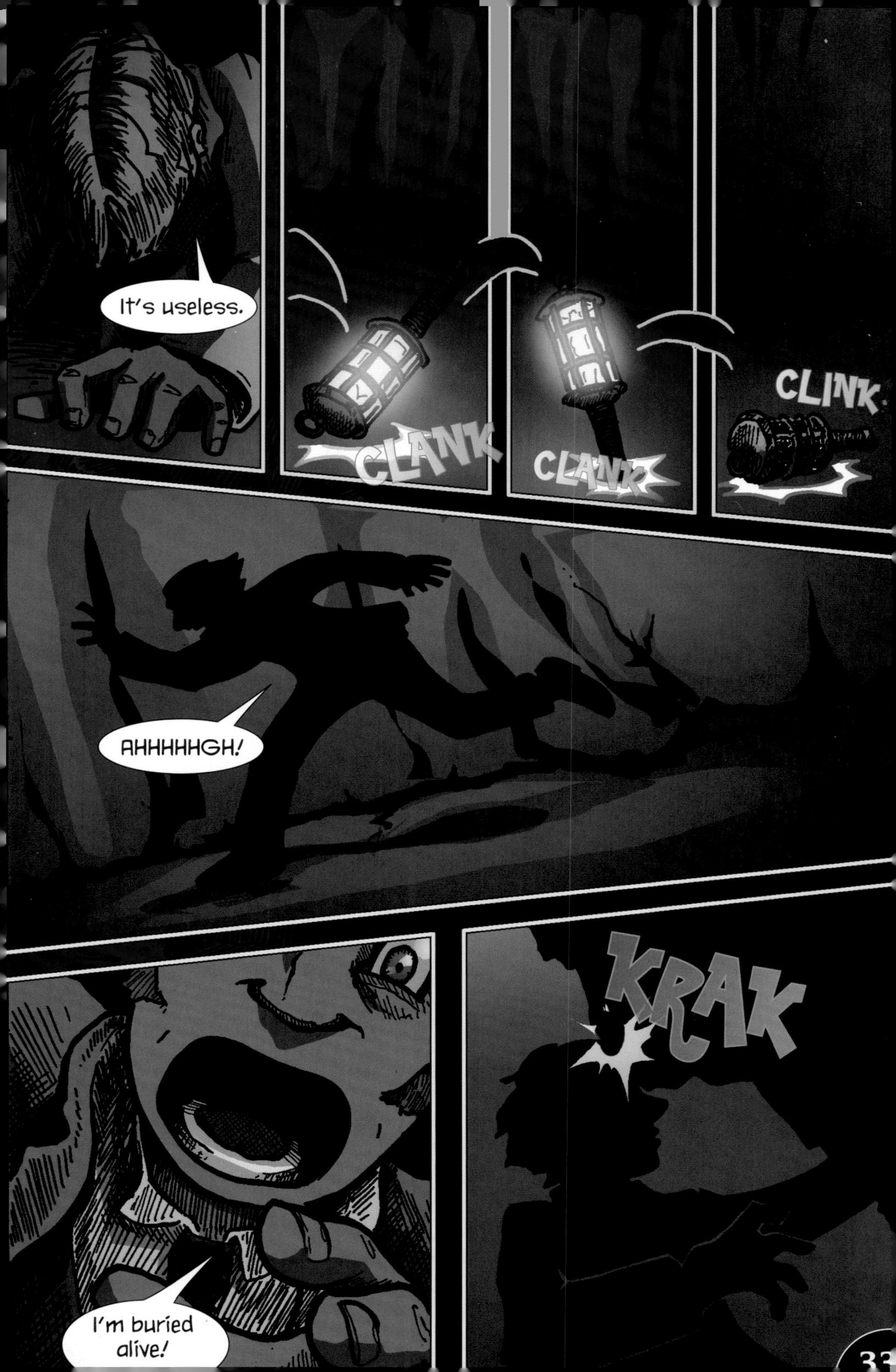
It's useless.
CLANK
CLANK
CLINK.
AHHHHHGH!
I'm buried alive!
KRAK

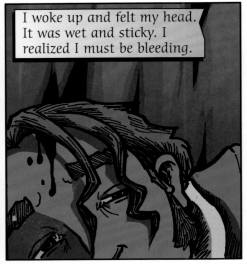

I woke up and felt my head. It was wet and sticky. I realized I must be bleeding.

What was that?

BANG

The sound had to be my uncle firing one of the rifles, hoping I'd hear him.

Uncle! Uncle Lidenbrock!

Axel, my boy!

Where are you?

I'm lost! And I can't see! My lamp is out!

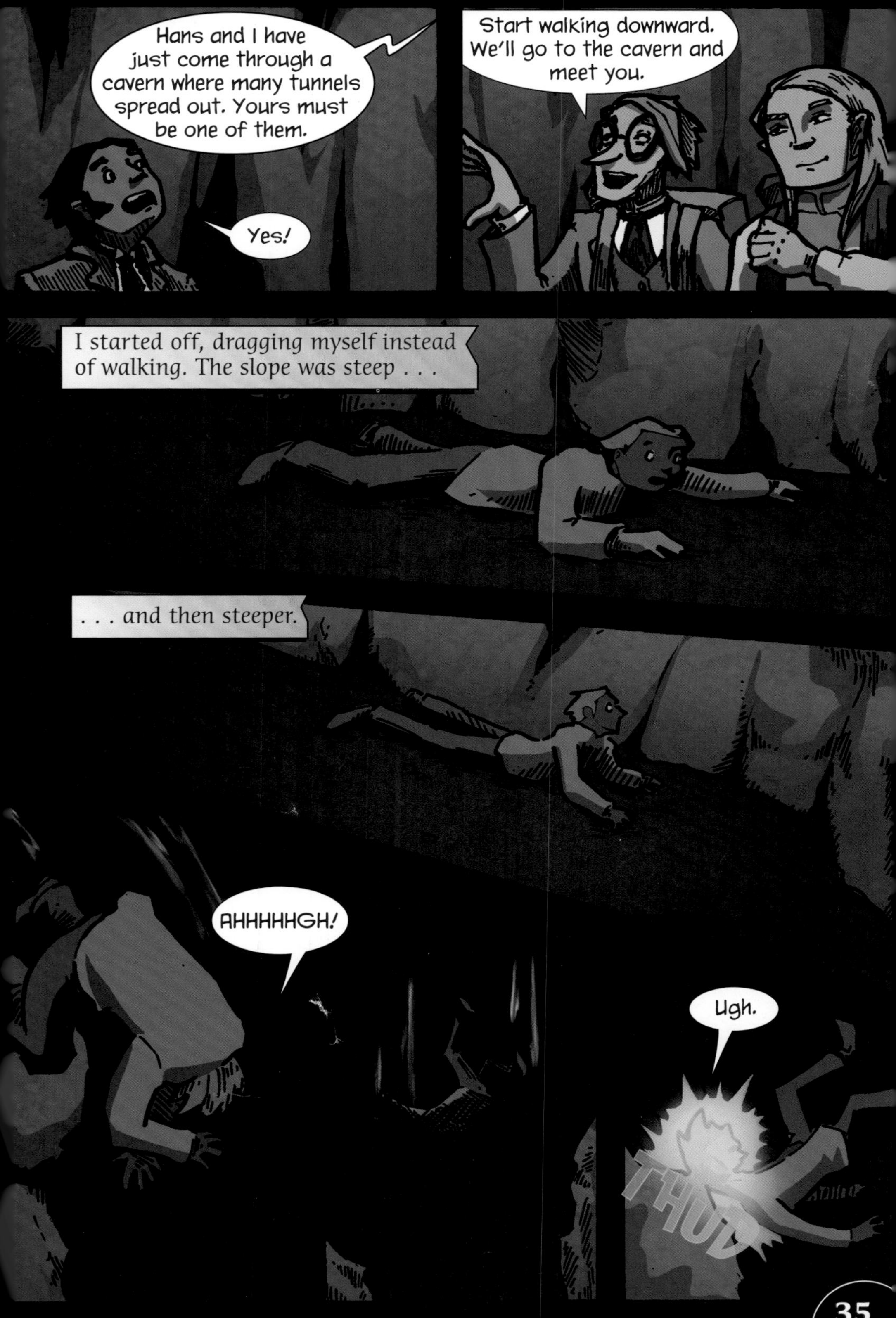
Hans and I have just come through a cavern where many tunnels spread out. Yours must be one of them.
Yes!
Start walking downward. We'll go to the cavern and meet you.
I started off, dragging myself instead of walking. The slope was steep . . .
. . . and then steeper.
AHHHHHGH!
Ugh.
THUD

CHAPTER 5 THE GREAT SEA

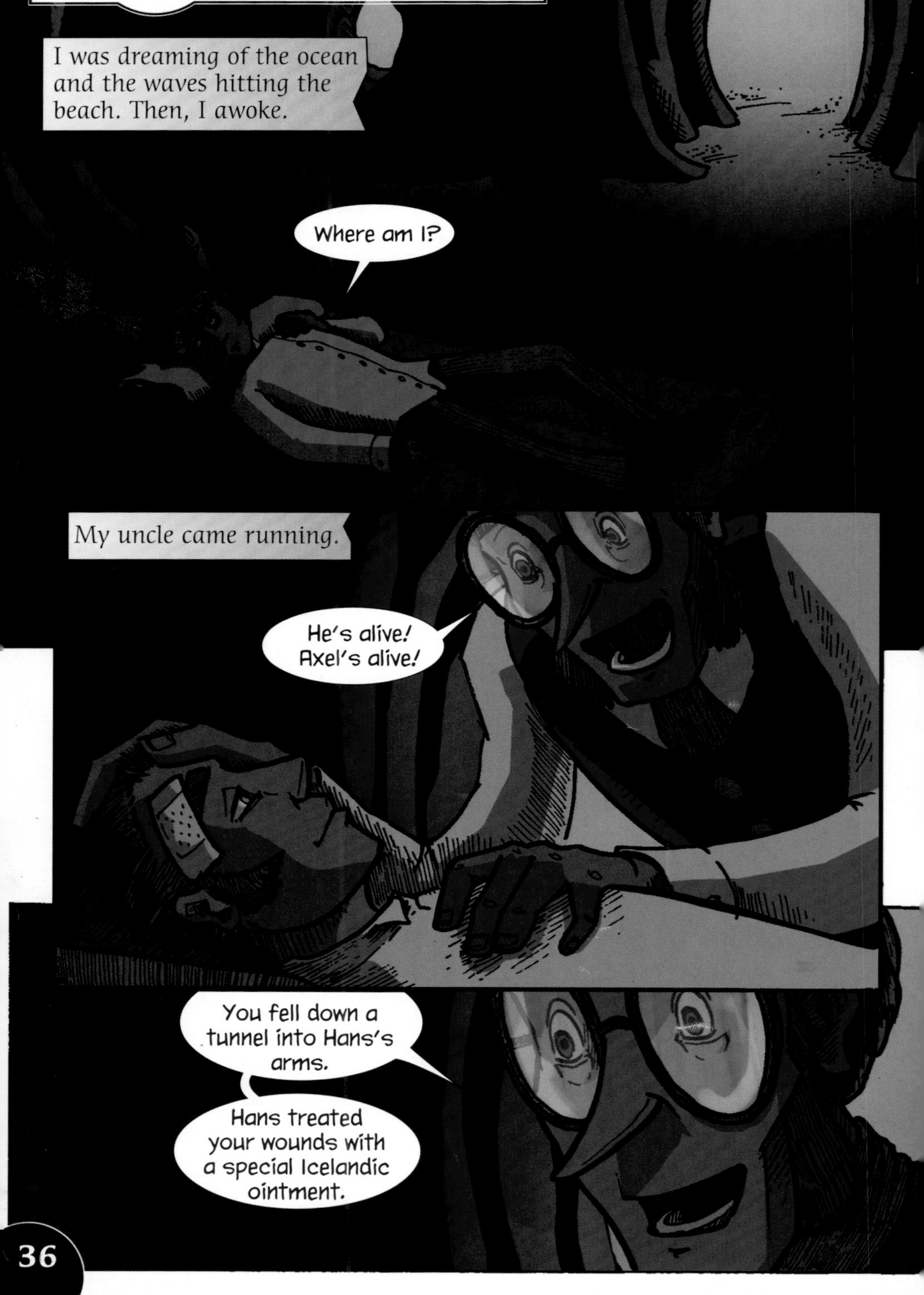
I was dreaming of the ocean and the waves hitting the beach. Then, I awoke.
Where am I?
My uncle came running.
He's alive! Axel's alive!
You fell down a tunnel into Hans's arms.
Hans treated your wounds with a special Icelandic ointment.

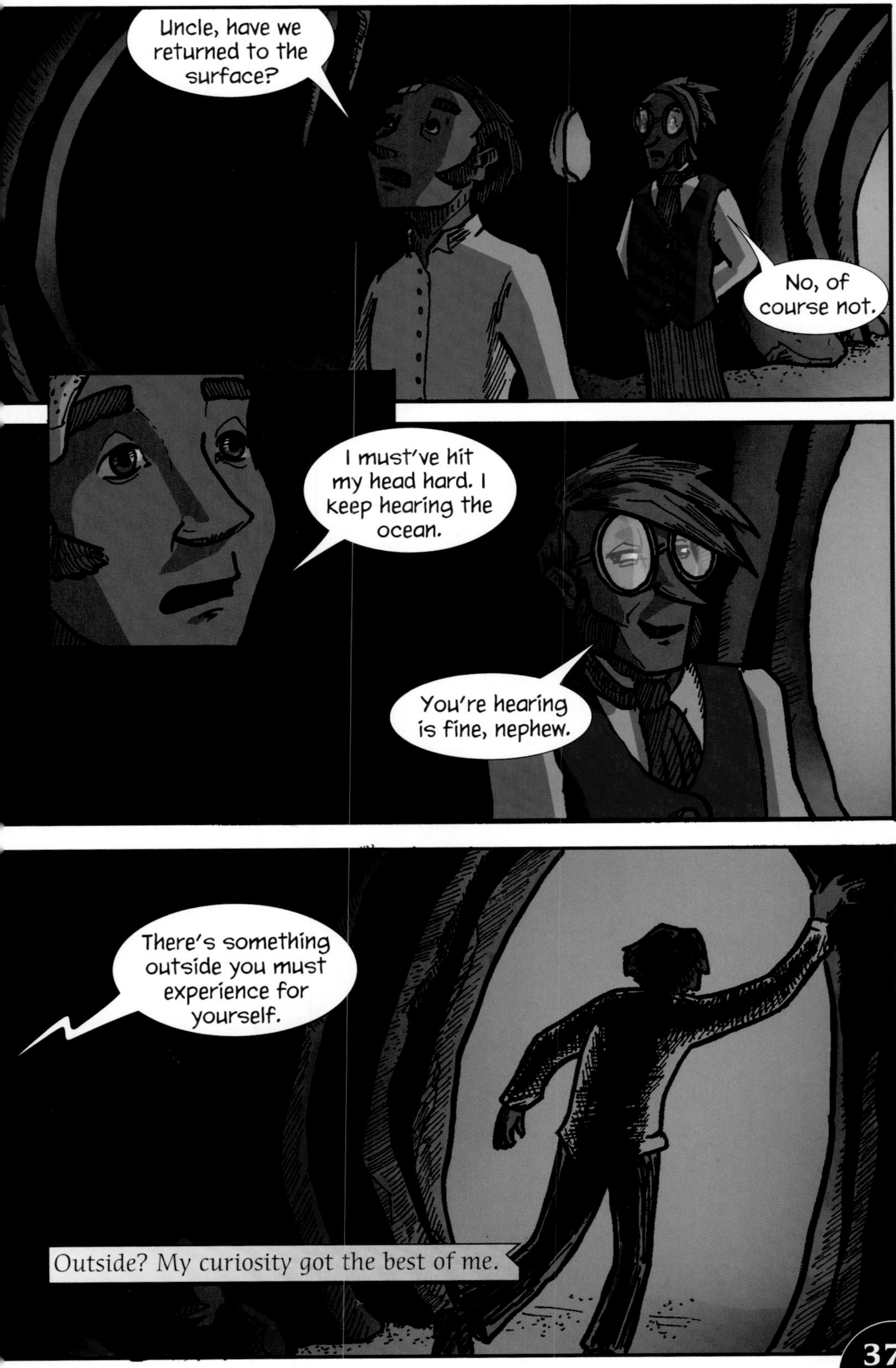

Uncle, have we returned to the surface?
No, of course not.
I must've hit my head hard. I keep hearing the ocean.
You're hearing is fine, nephew.
There's something outside you must experience for yourself.
Outside? My curiosity got the best of me.

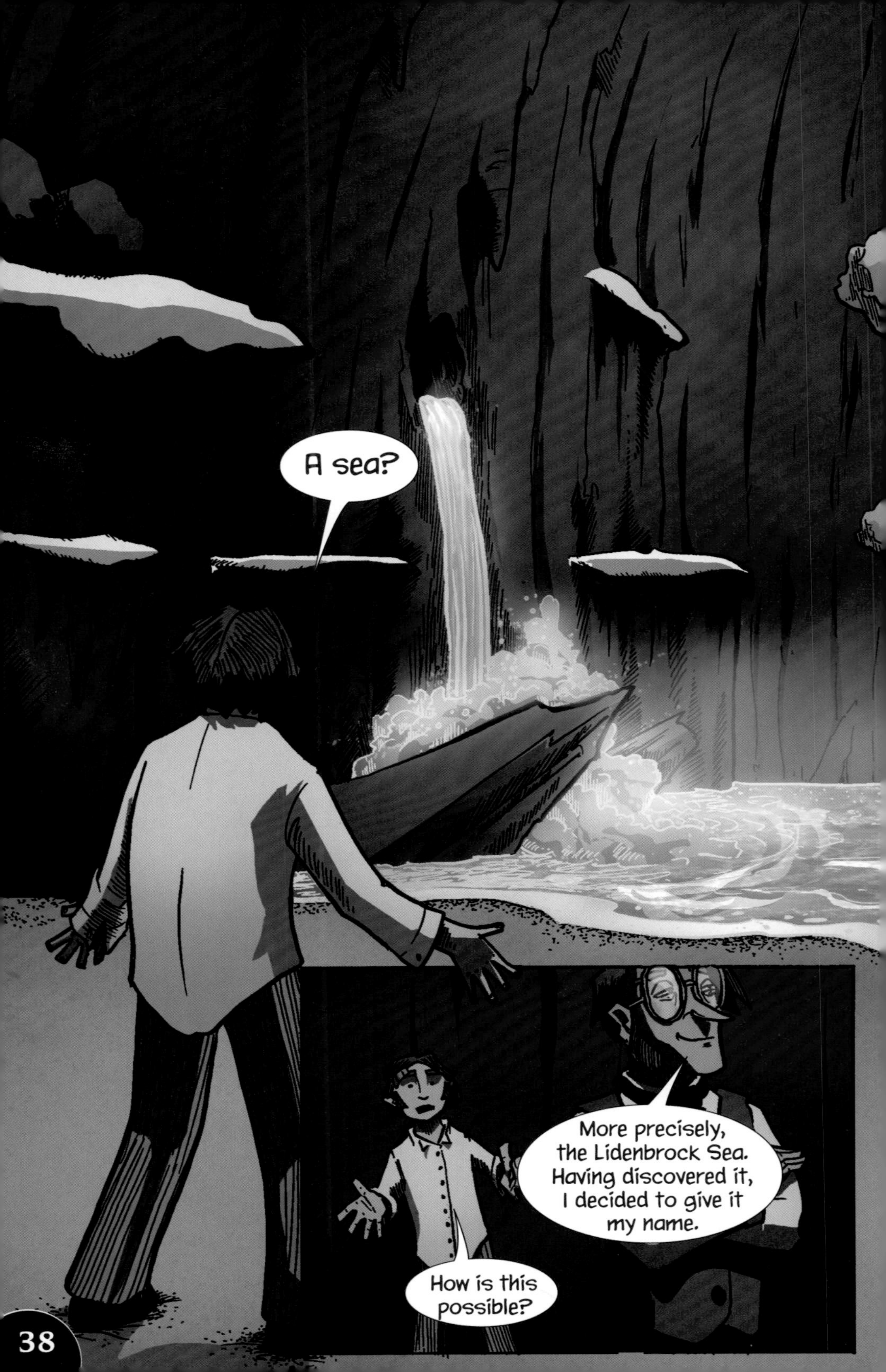
A sea?
More precisely, the Lidenbrock Sea. Having discovered it, I decided to give it my name.
How is this possible?

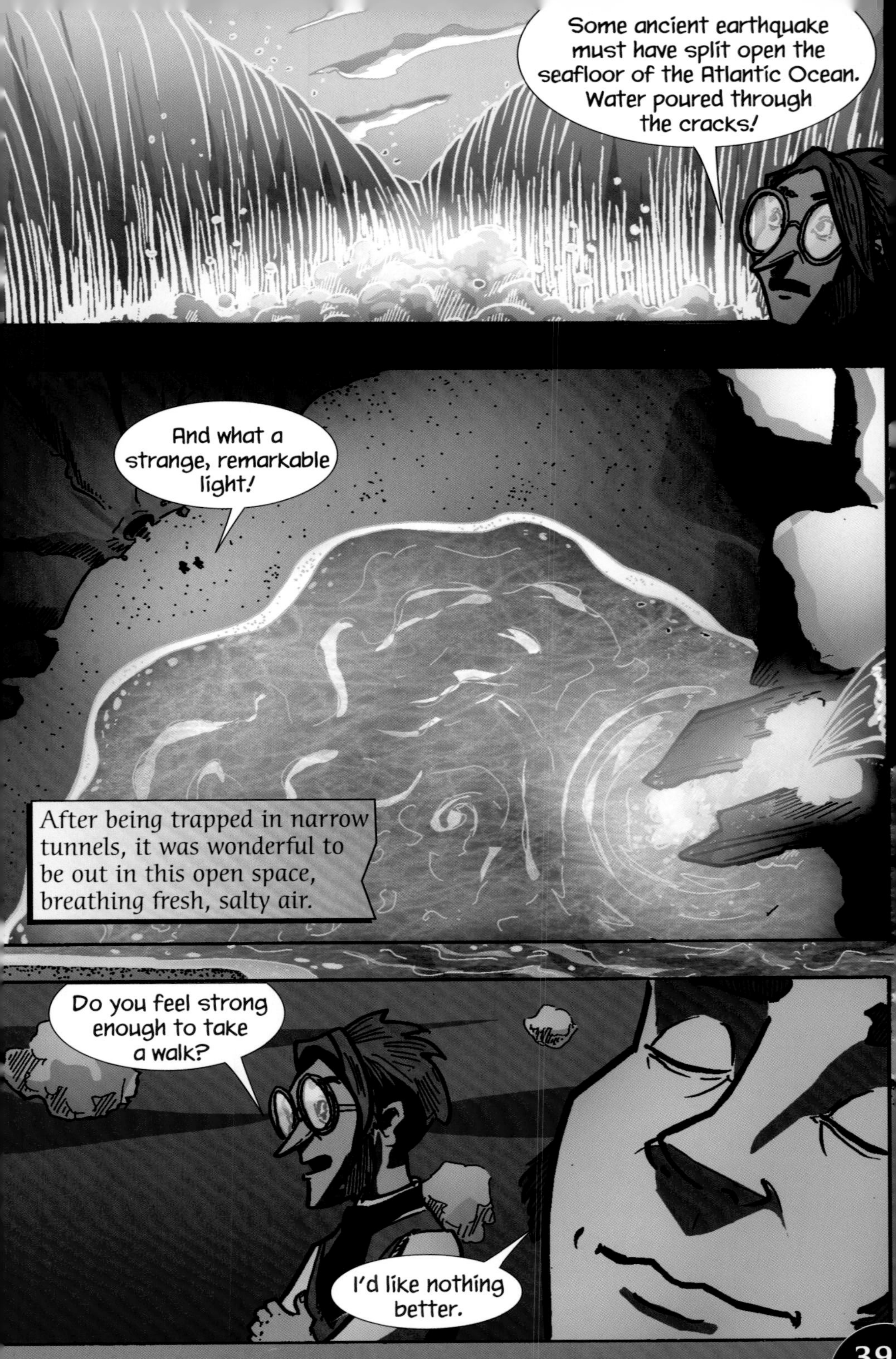

Some ancient earthquake must have split open the seafloor of the Atlantic Ocean. Water poured through the cracks!
And what a strange, remarkable light!
After being trapped in narrow tunnels, it was wonderful to be out in this open space, breathing fresh, salty air.
Do you feel strong enough to take a walk?
I'd like nothing better.

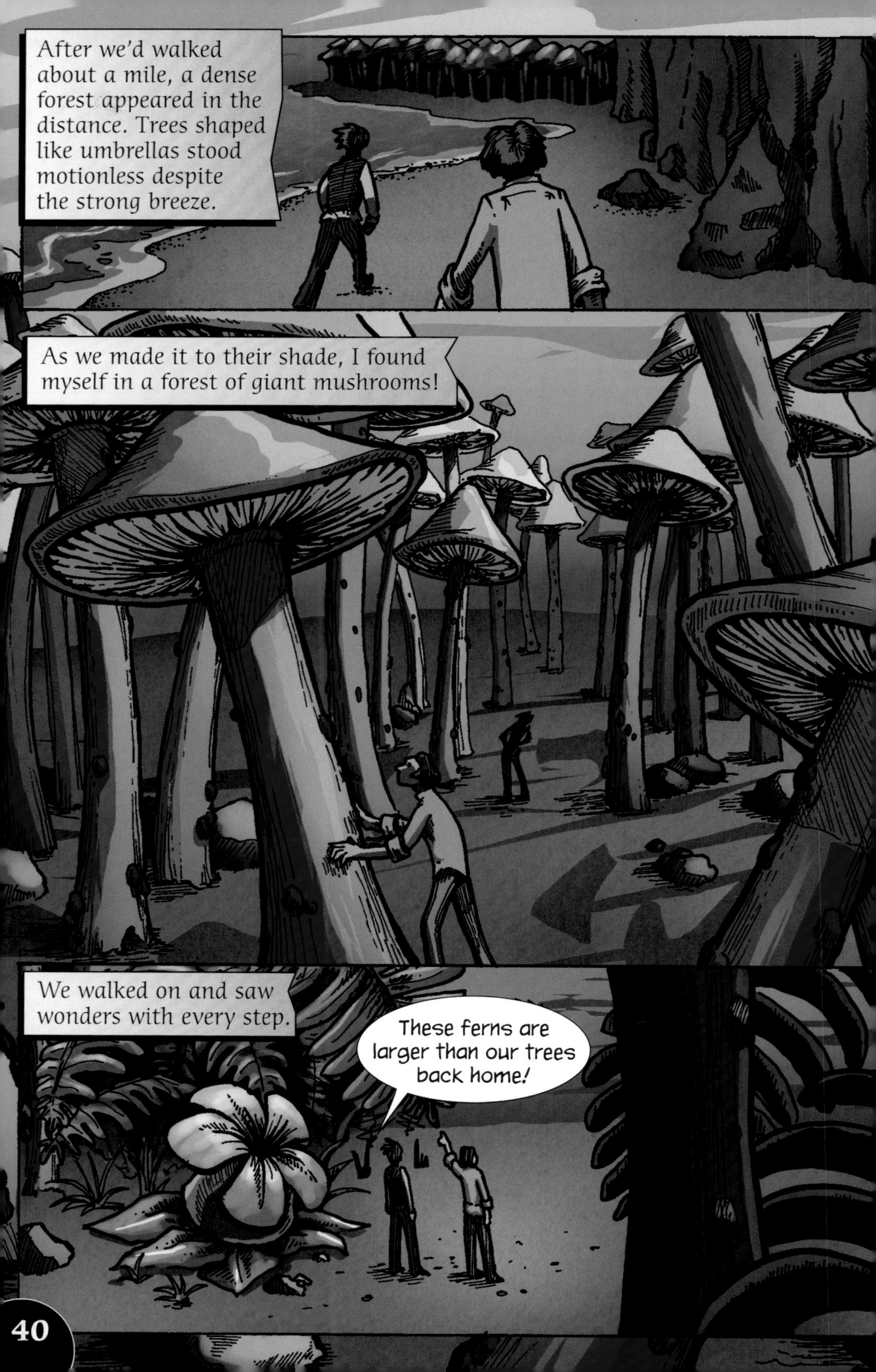
After we'd walked about a mile, a dense forest appeared in the distance. Trees shaped like umbrellas stood motionless despite the strong breeze.
As we made it to their shade, I found myself in a forest of giant mushrooms!
We walked on and saw wonders with every step.
These ferns are larger than our trees back home!

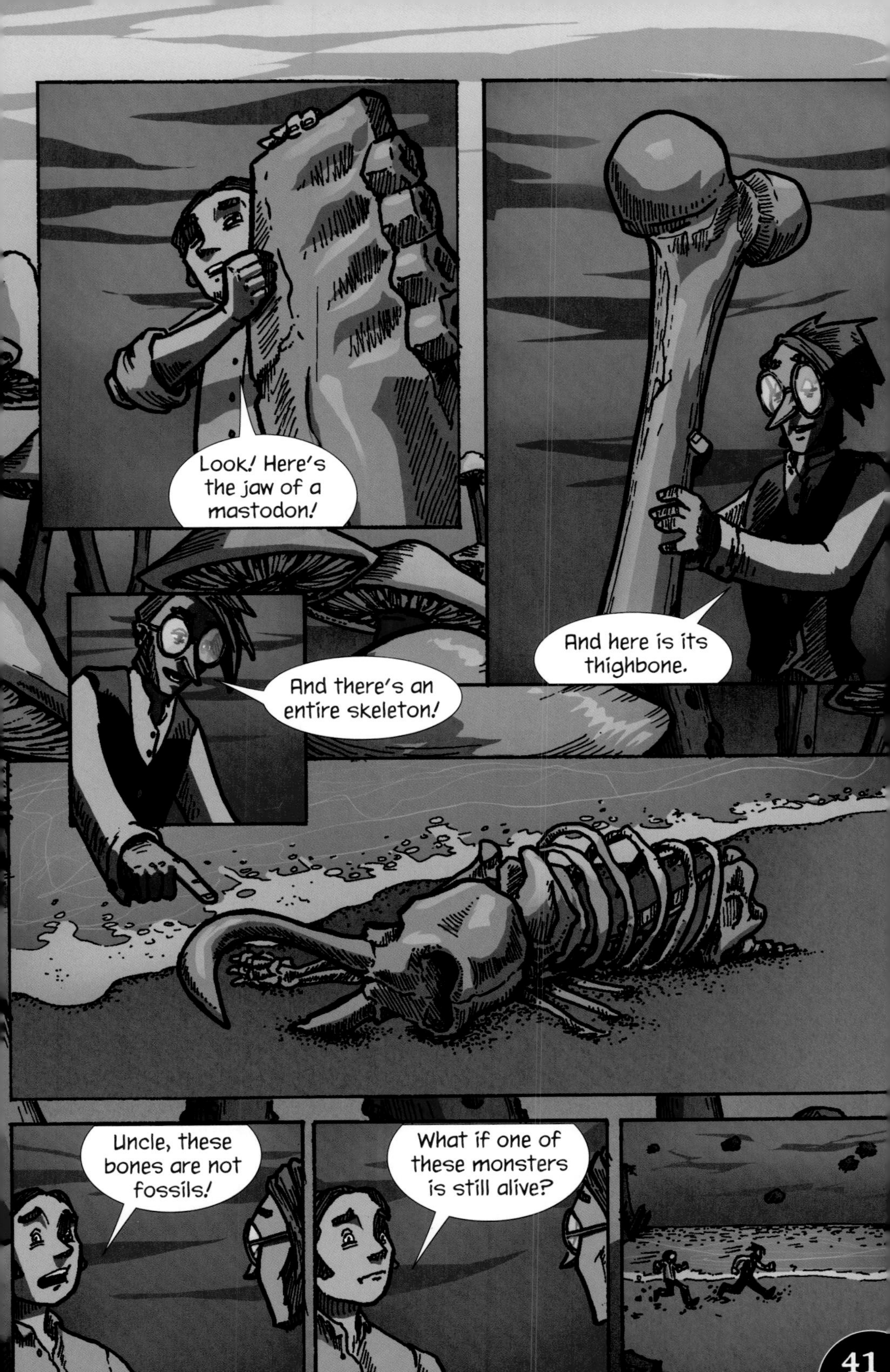
Look! Here's the jaw of a mastodon!
And here is its thighbone.
And there's an entire skeleton!
Uncle, these bones are not fossils!
What if one of these monsters is still alive?

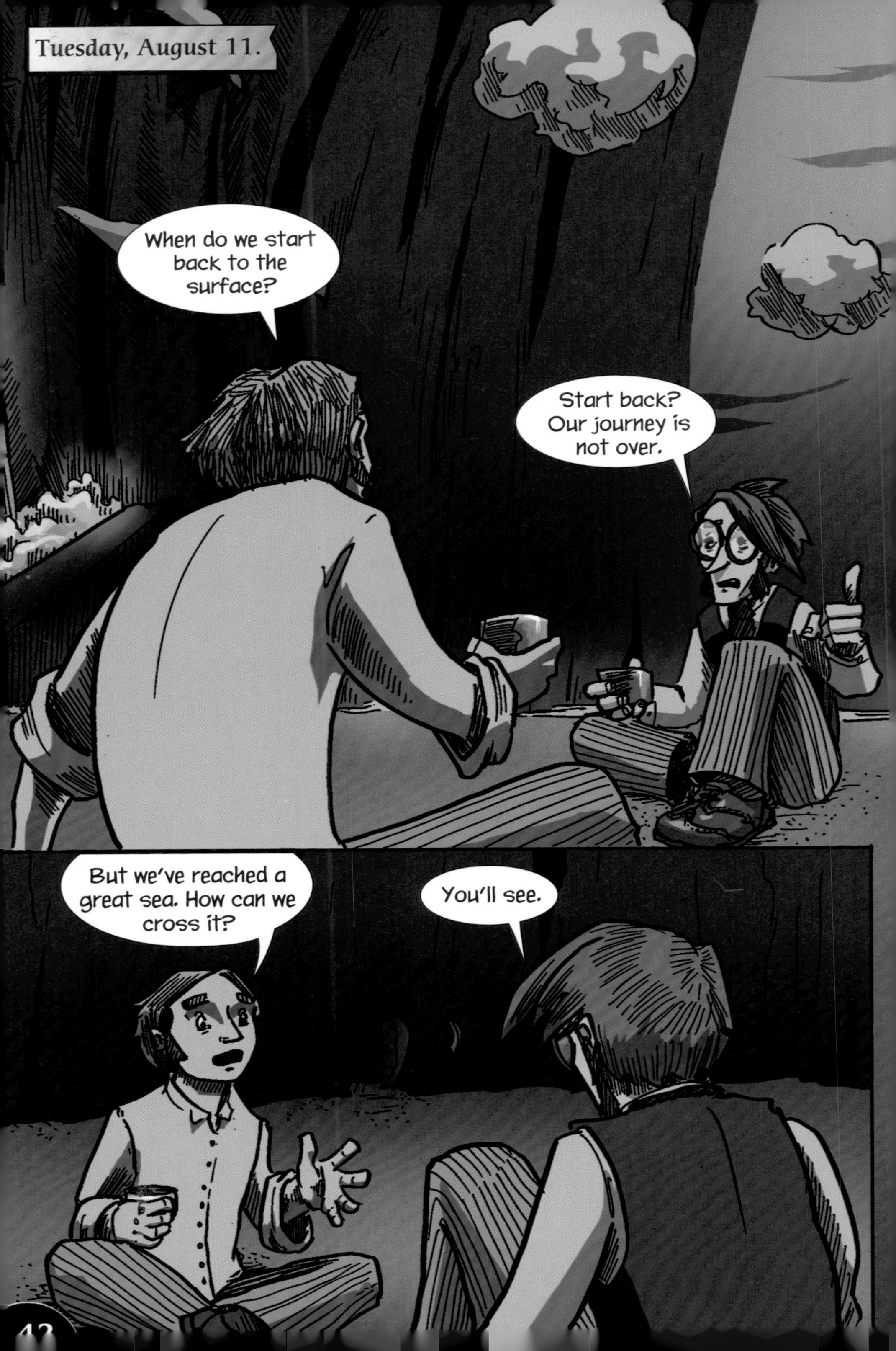
Tuesday, August 11.
When do we start back to the surface?
Start back? Our journey is not over.
But we've reached a great sea. How can we cross it?
You'll see.

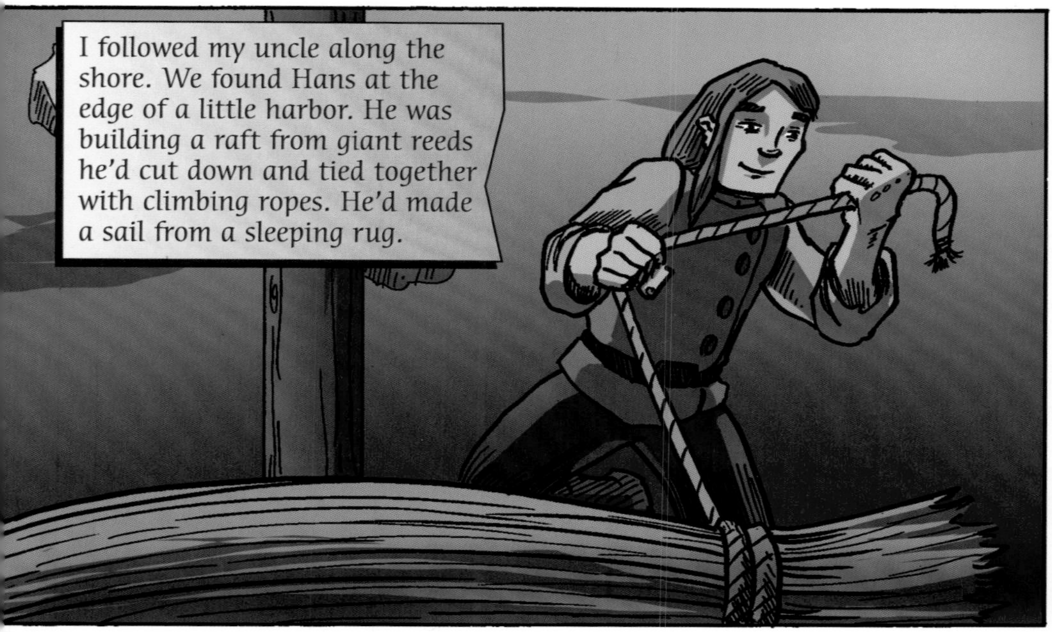
I followed my uncle along the shore. We found Hans at the edge of a little harbor. He was building a raft from giant reeds he'd cut down and tied together with climbing ropes. He'd made a sail from a sleeping rug.

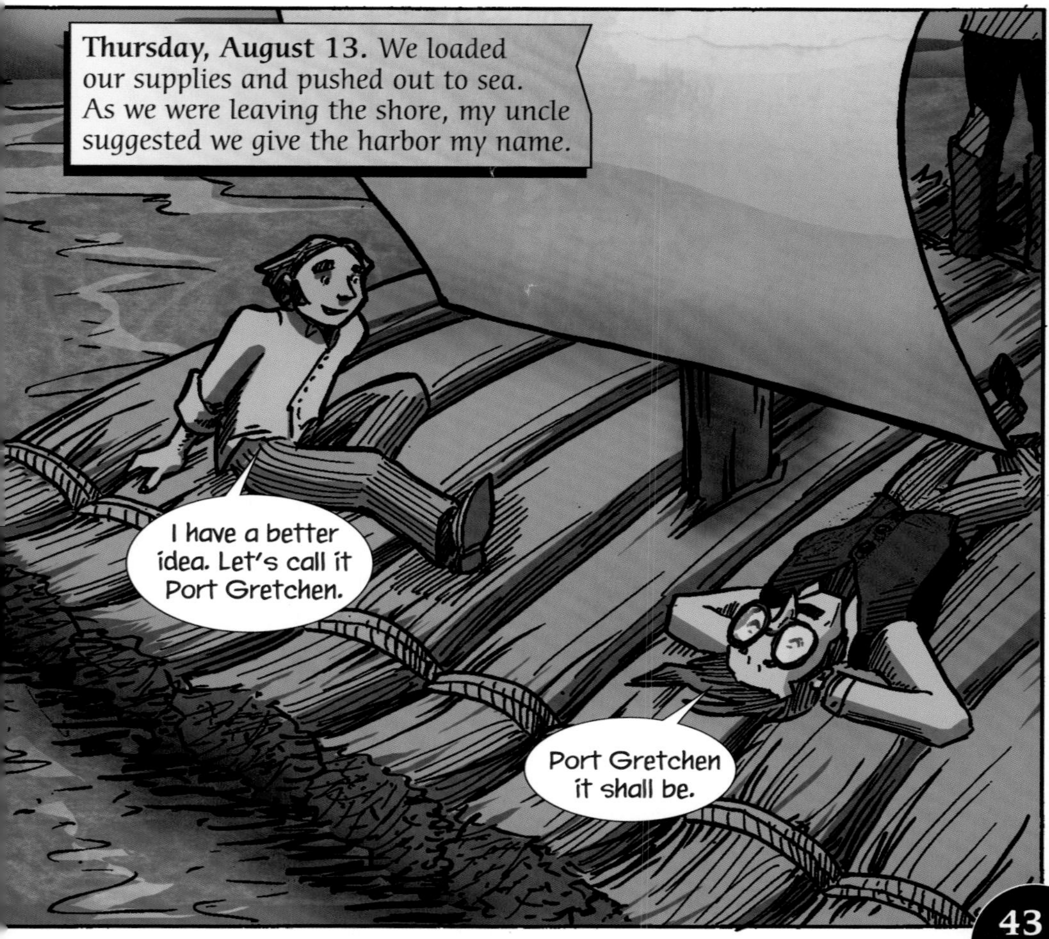
Thursday, August 13. We loaded our supplies and pushed out to sea. As we were leaving the shore, my uncle suggested we give the harbor my name.
I have a better idea. Let's call it Port Gretchen.
Port Gretchen it shall be.

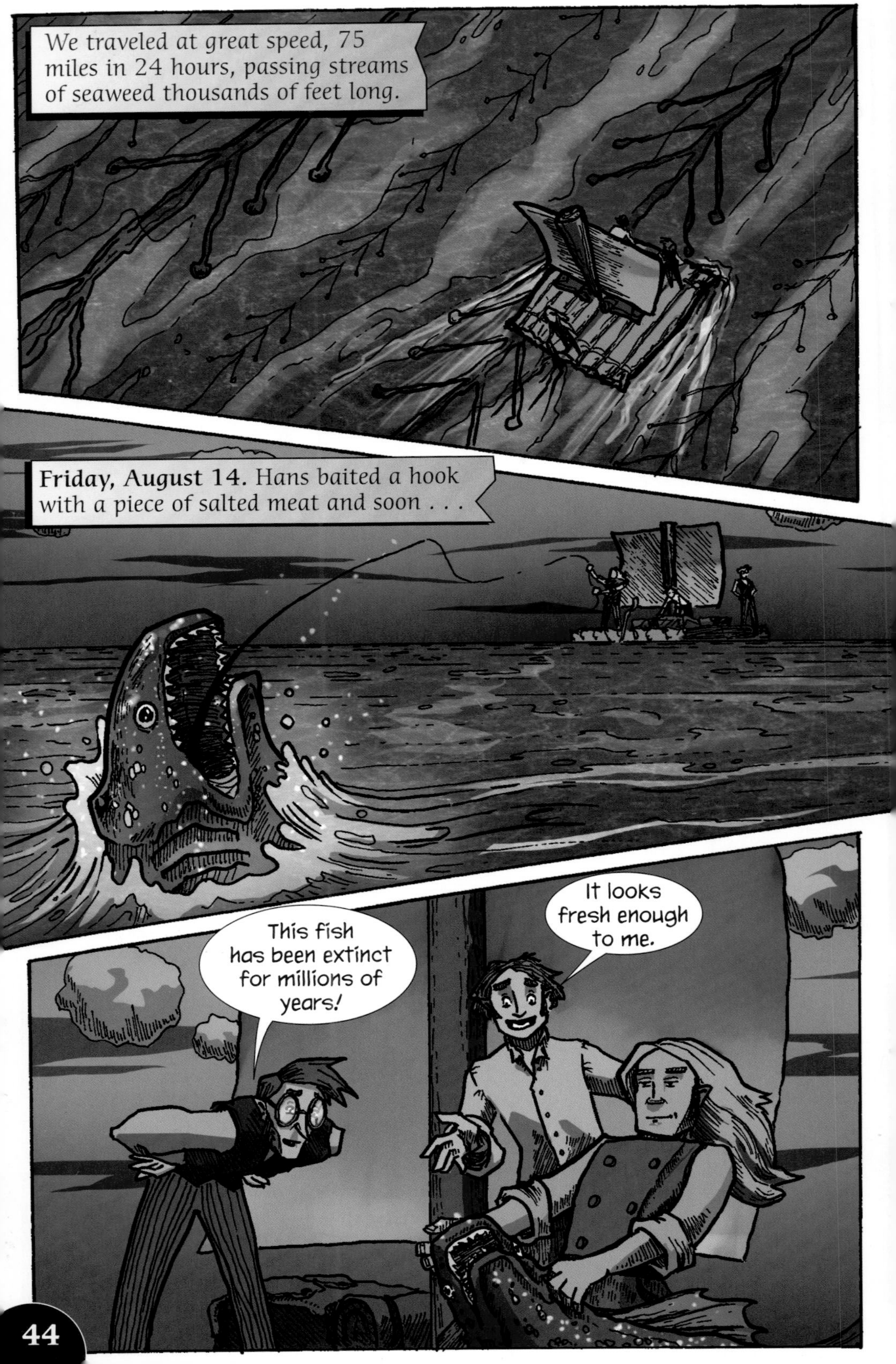
We traveled at great speed, 75 miles in 24 hours, passing streams of seaweed thousands of feet long.
Friday, August 14. Hans baited a hook with a piece of salted meat and soon . . .
This fish has been extinct for millions of years!
It looks fresh enough to me.

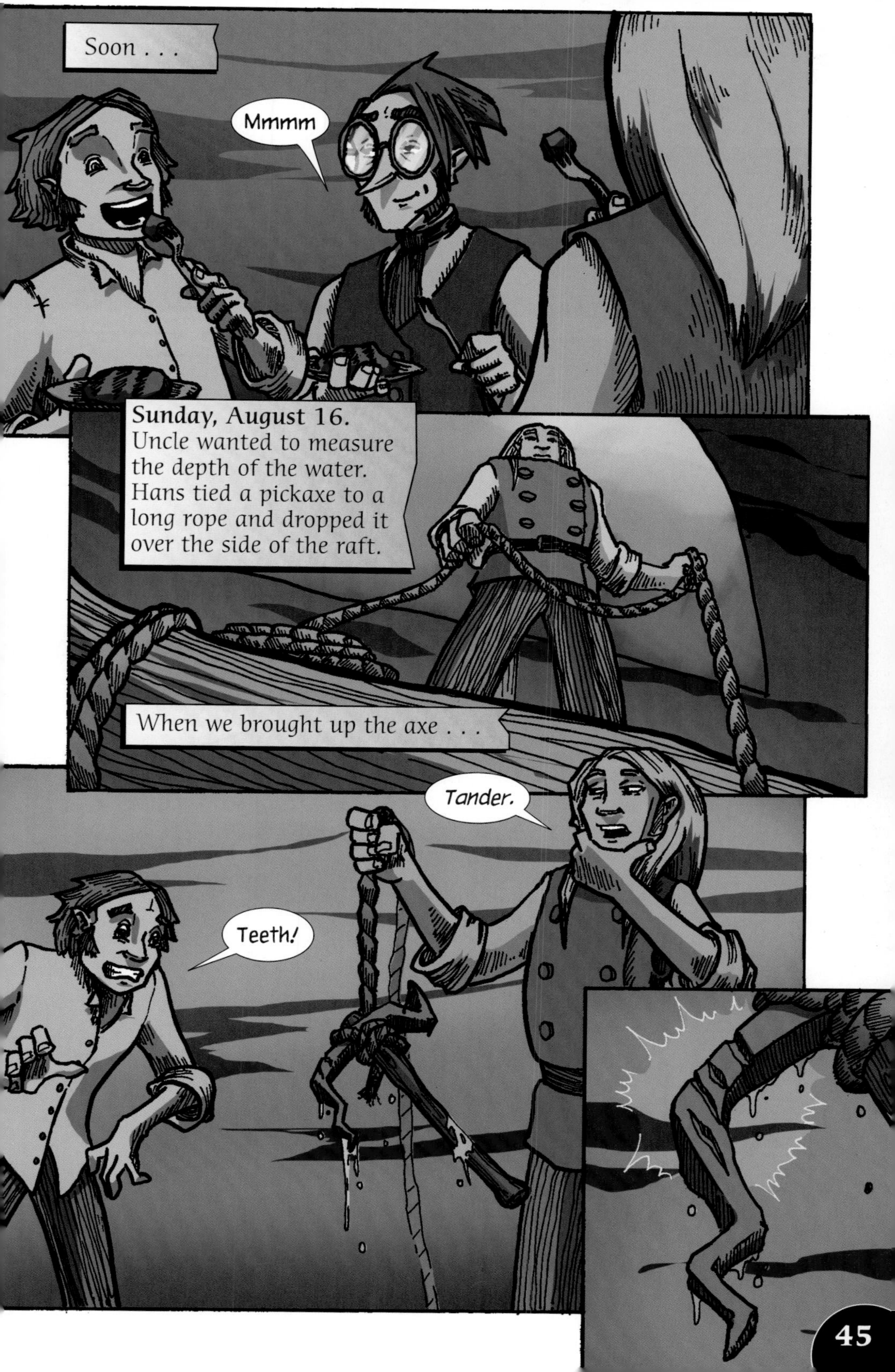
Soon . . .
Mmmm
Sunday, August 16.
Uncle wanted to measure the depth of the water. Hans tied a pickaxe to a long rope and dropped it over the side of the raft.
When we brought up the axe . . .
Tander.
Teeth!

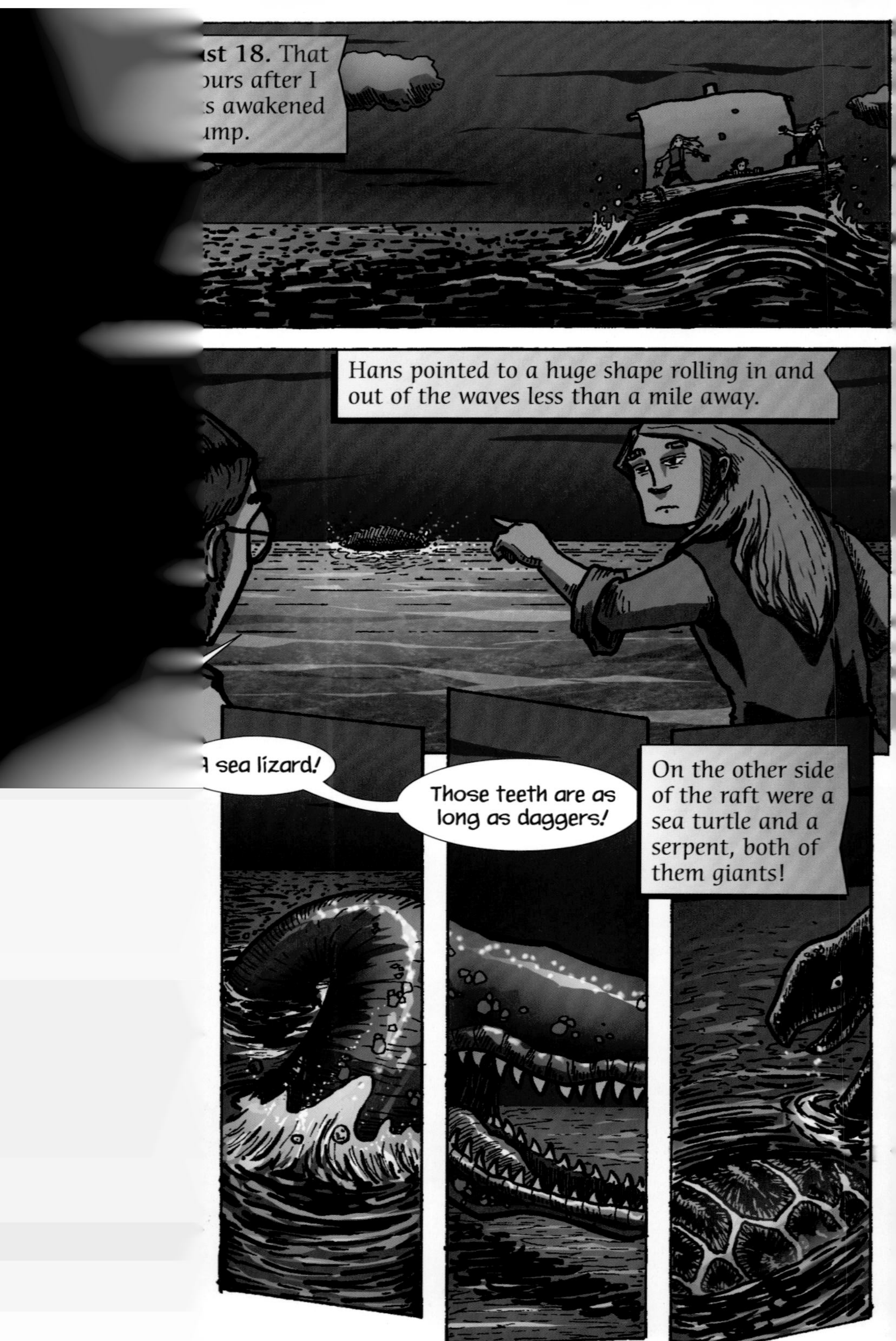
st 18. That
ours after I
s awakened
ump.
Hans pointed to a huge shape rolling in and out of the waves less than a mile away.
A sea lizard!
Those teeth are as long as daggers!
On the other side of the raft were a sea turtle and a serpent, both of them giants!

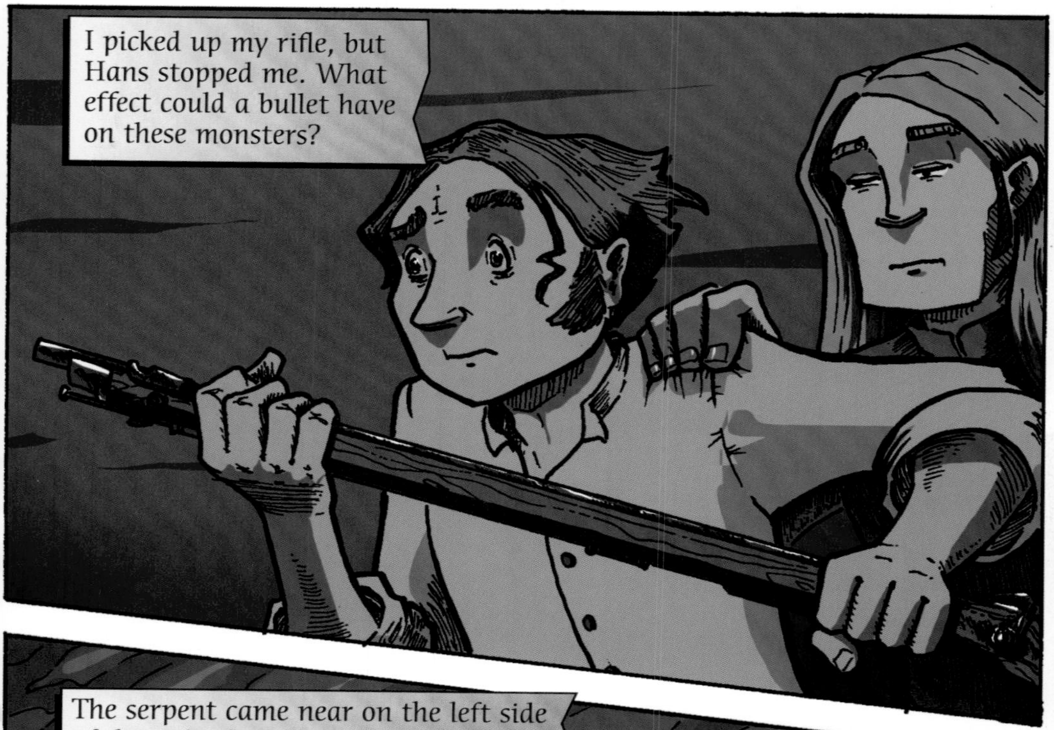
I picked up my rifle, but Hans stopped me. What effect could a bullet have on these monsters?

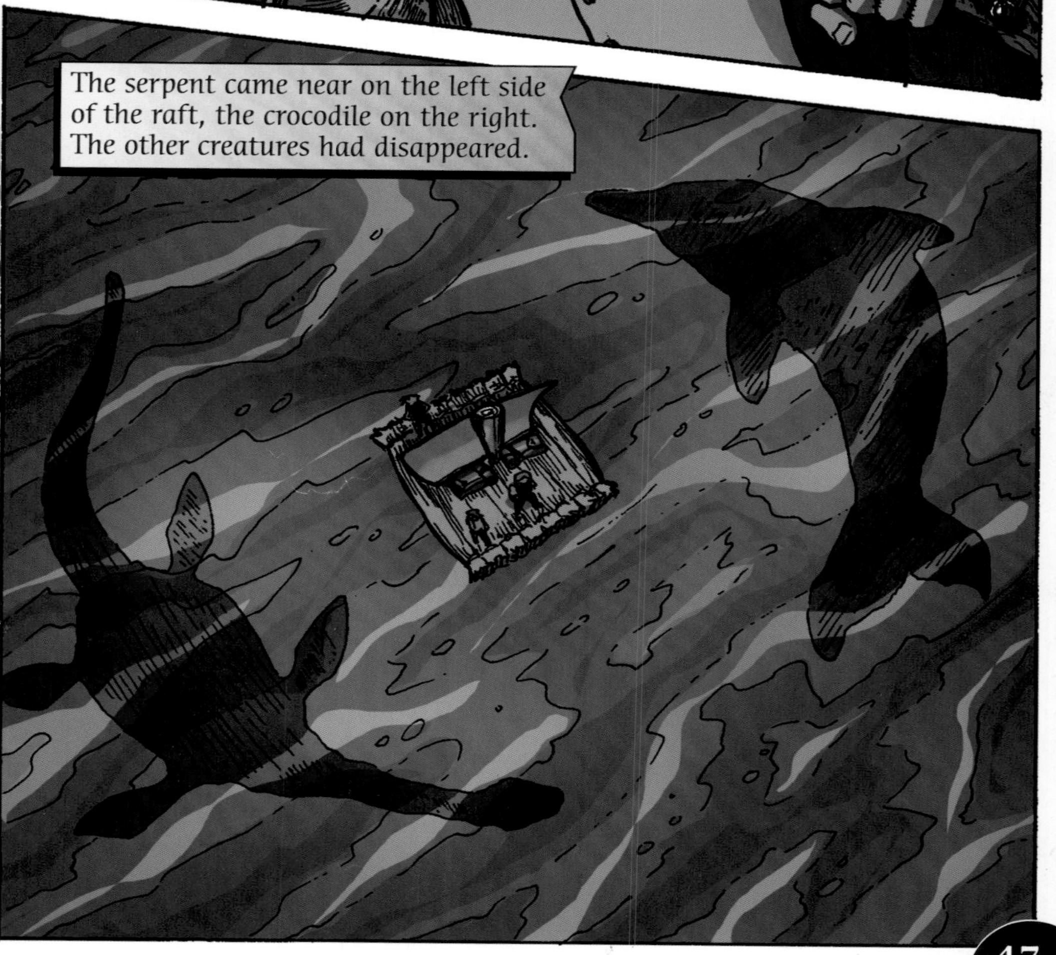
The serpent came near on the left side of the raft, the crocodile on the right. The other creatures had disappeared.

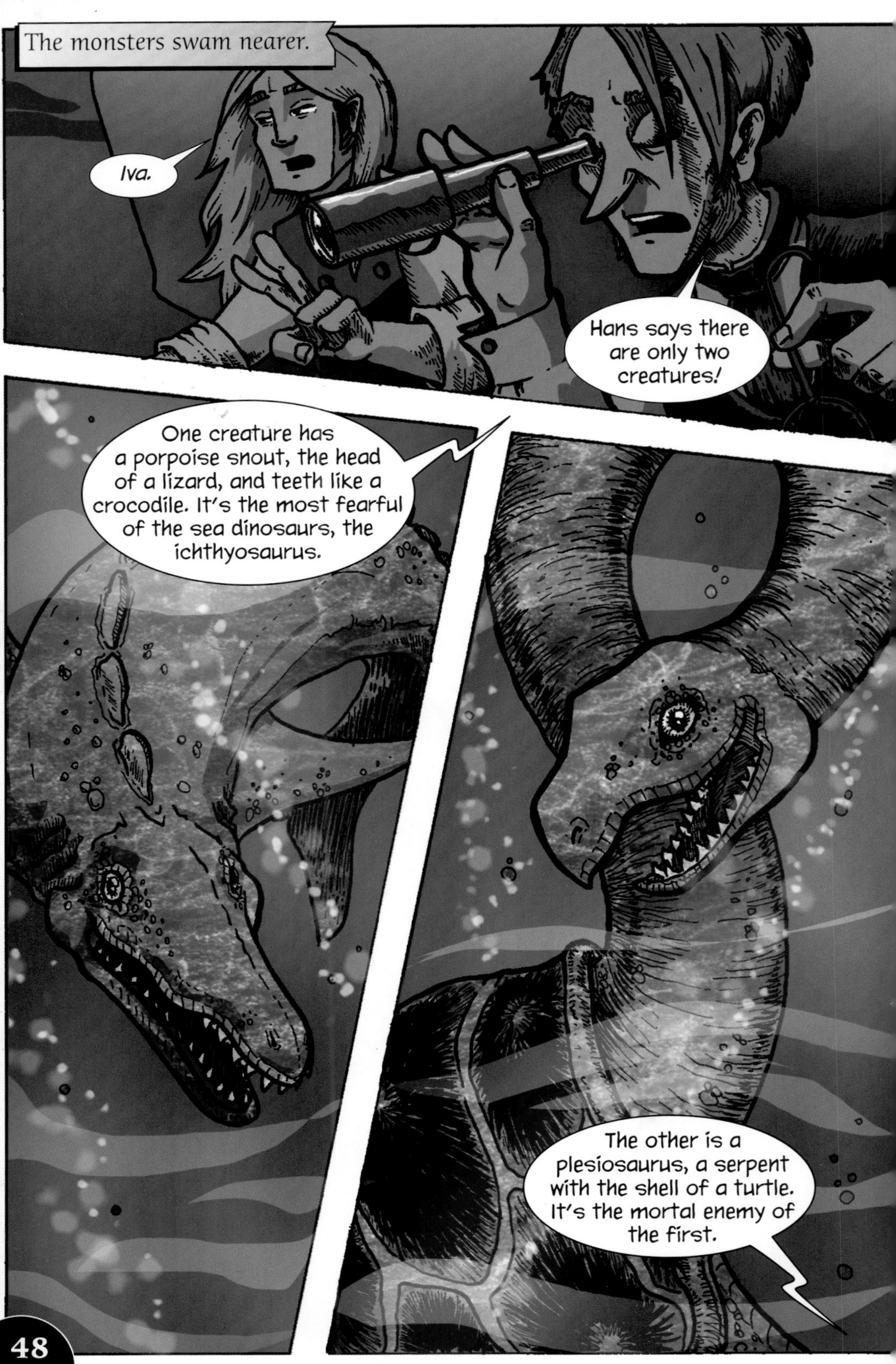
The monsters swam nearer.
Iva.
Hans says there are only two creatures!
One creature has a porpoise snout, the head of a lizard, and teeth like a crocodile. It's the most fearful of the sea dinosaurs, the ichthyosaurus.
The other is a plesiosaurus, a serpent with the shell of a turtle. It's the mortal enemy of the first.

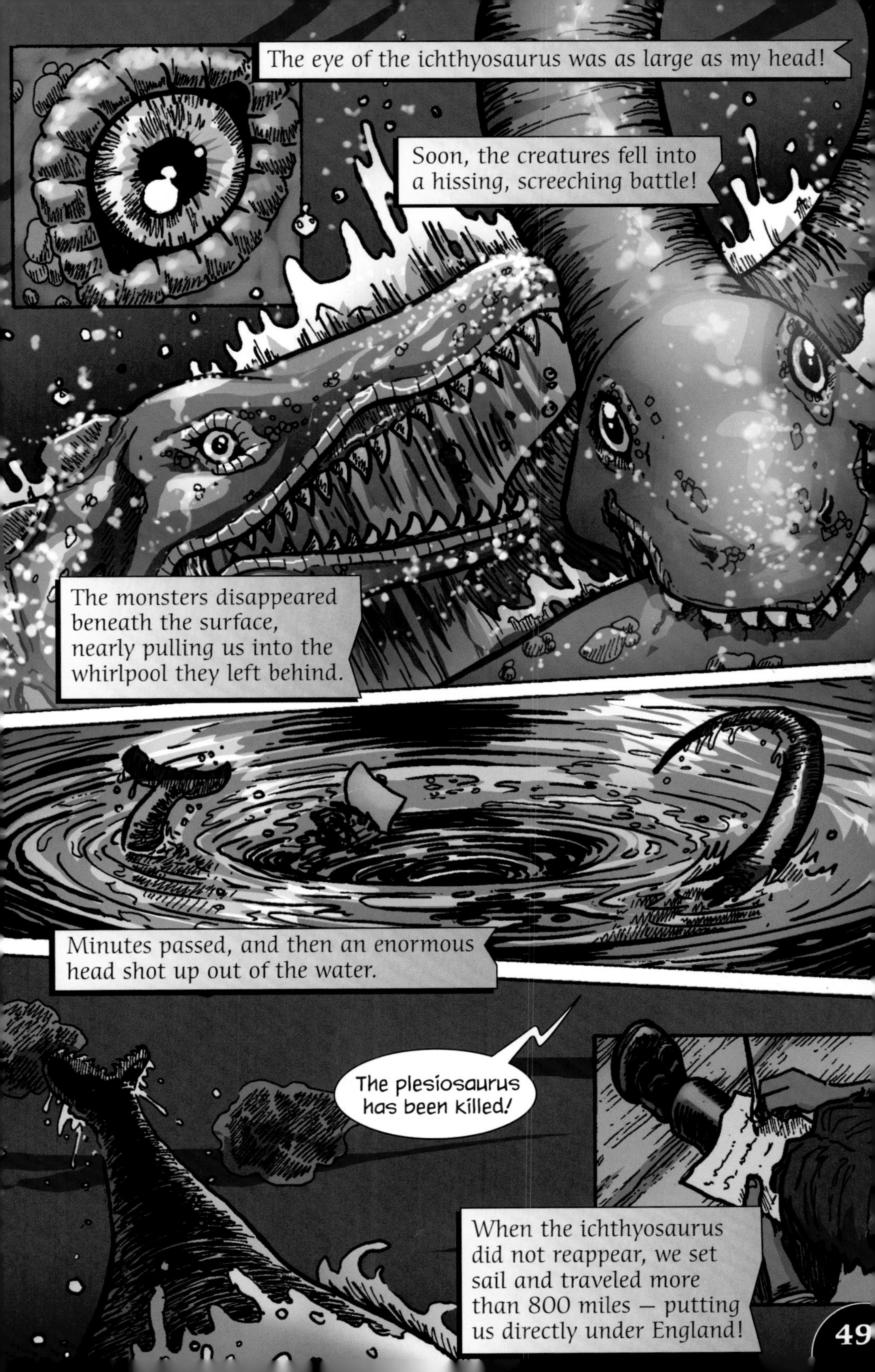
The eye of the ichthyosaurus was as large as my head!
Soon, the creatures fell into a hissing, screeching battle!
The monsters disappeared beneath the surface, nearly pulling us into the whirlpool they left behind.
Minutes passed, and then an enormous head shot up out of the water.
The plesiosaurus has been killed!
When the ichthyosaurus did not reappear, we set sail and traveled more than 800 miles — putting us directly under England!

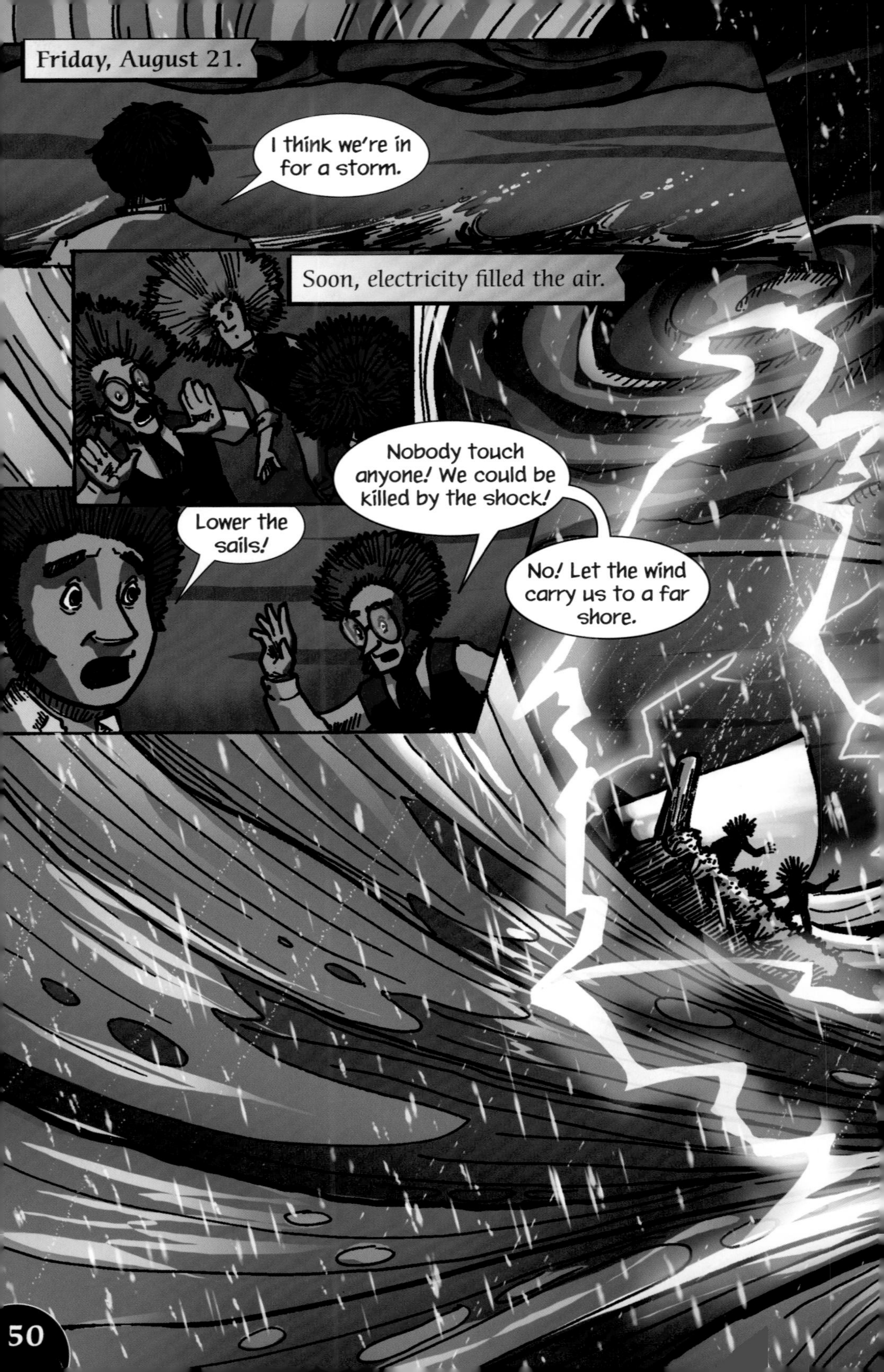
Friday, August 21.
I think we're in for a storm.
Soon, electricity filled the air.
Nobody touch anyone! We could be killed by the shock!
Lower the sails!
No! Let the wind carry us to a far shore.

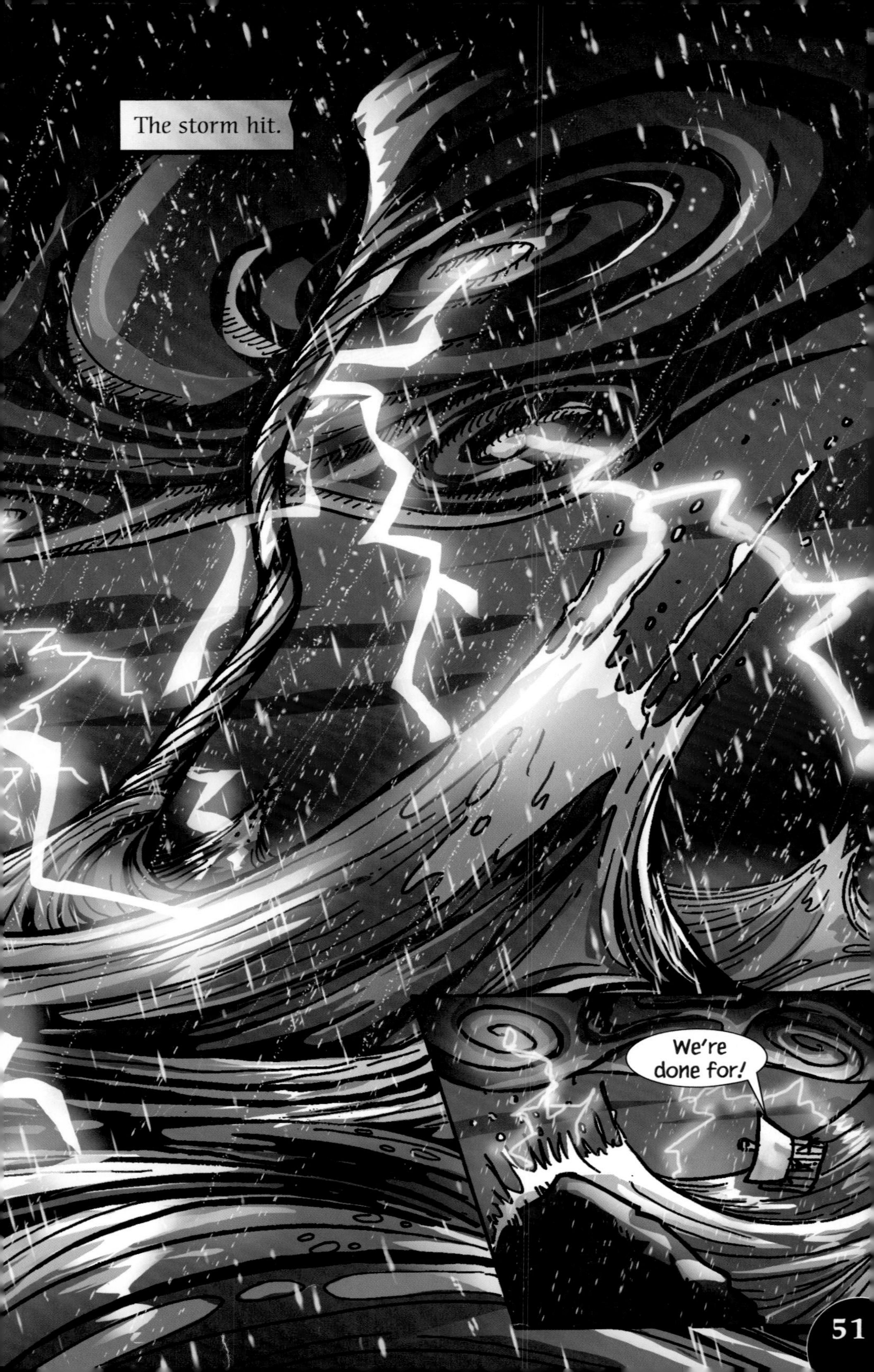
The storm hit.
We're done for!

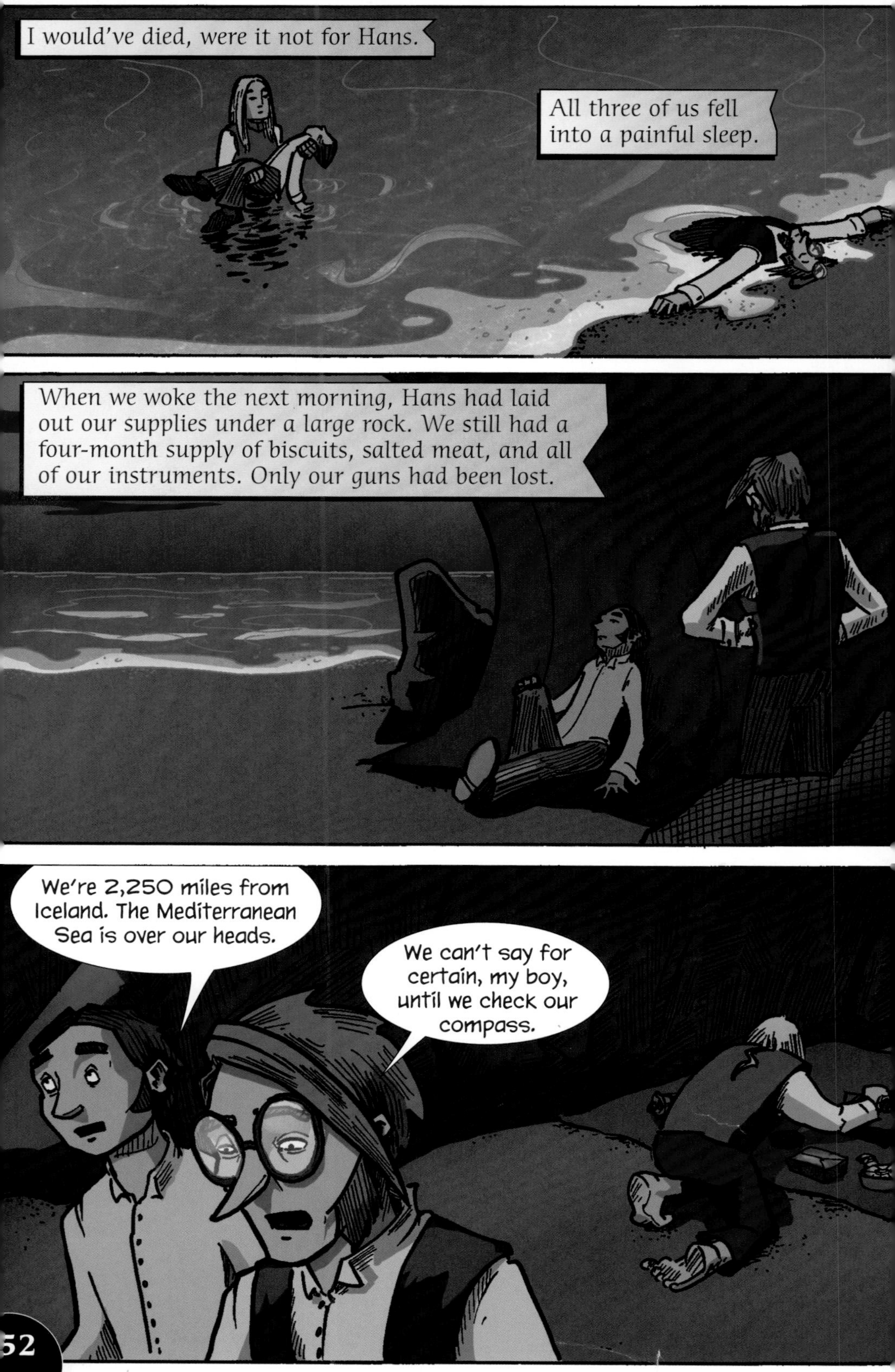
I would've died, were it not for Hans.
All three of us fell into a painful sleep.
When we woke the next morning, Hans had laid out our supplies under a large rock. We still had a four-month supply of biscuits, salted meat, and all of our instruments. Only our guns had been lost.
We're 2,250 miles from Iceland. The Mediterranean Sea is over our heads.
We can't say for certain, my boy, until we check our compass.

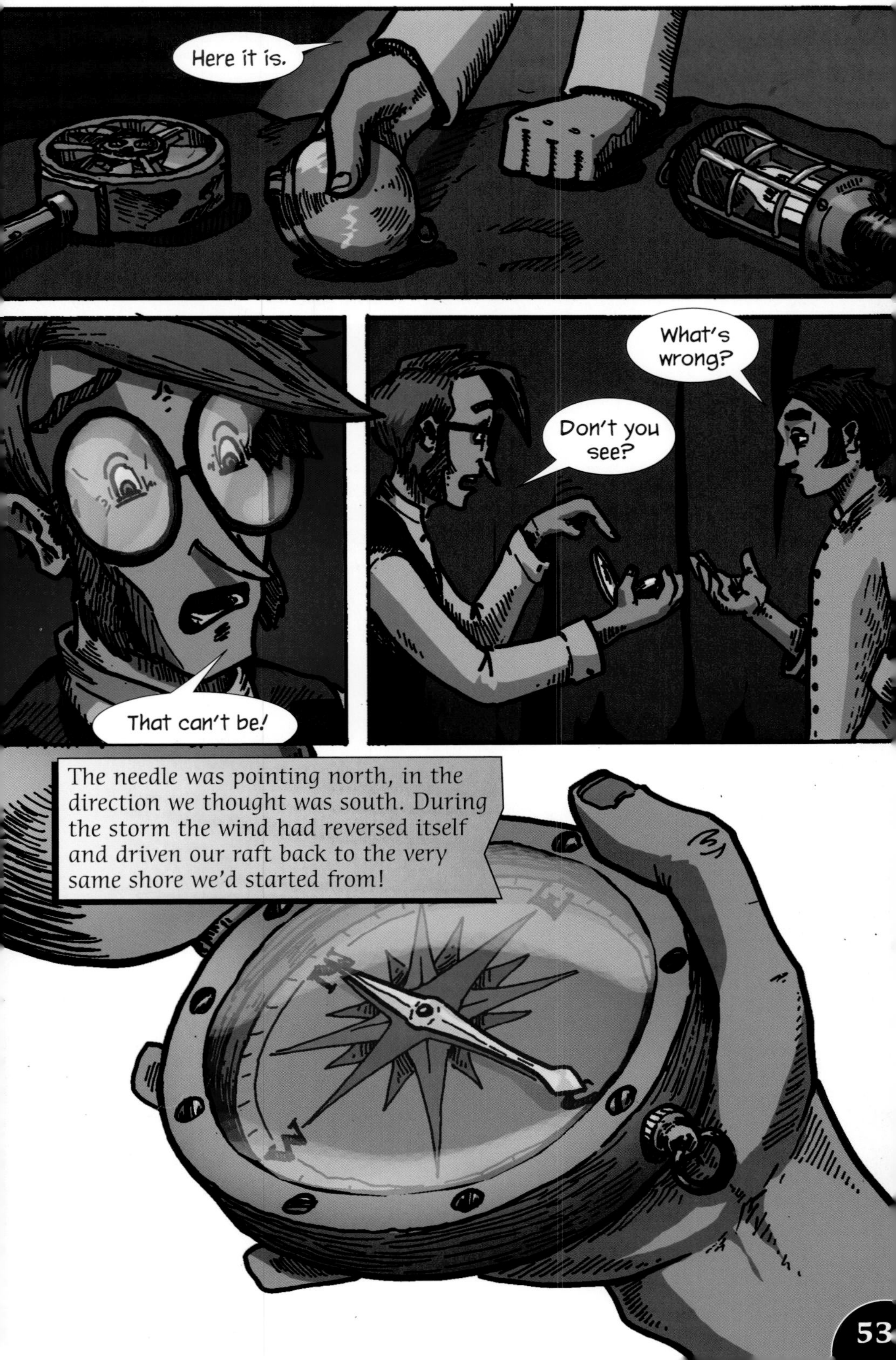
Here it is.
That can't be!
What's wrong?
Don't you see?
The needle was pointing north, in the direction we thought was south. During the storm the wind had reversed itself and driven our raft back to the very same shore we'd started from!

CHAPTER 6 THE BOILING TUNNEL

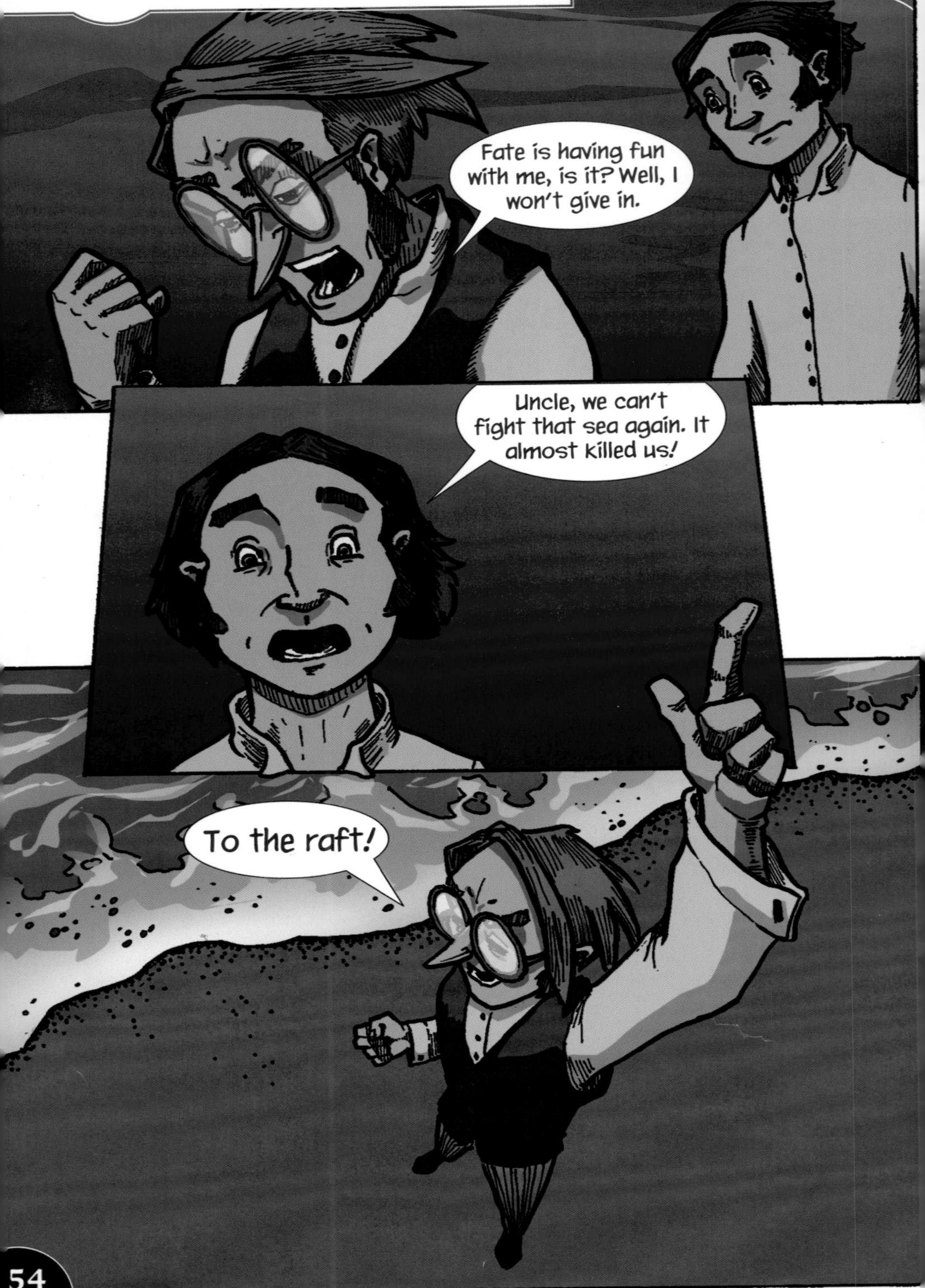
Fate is having fun with me, is it? Well, I won't give in.
Uncle, we can't fight that sea again. It almost killed us!
To the raft!

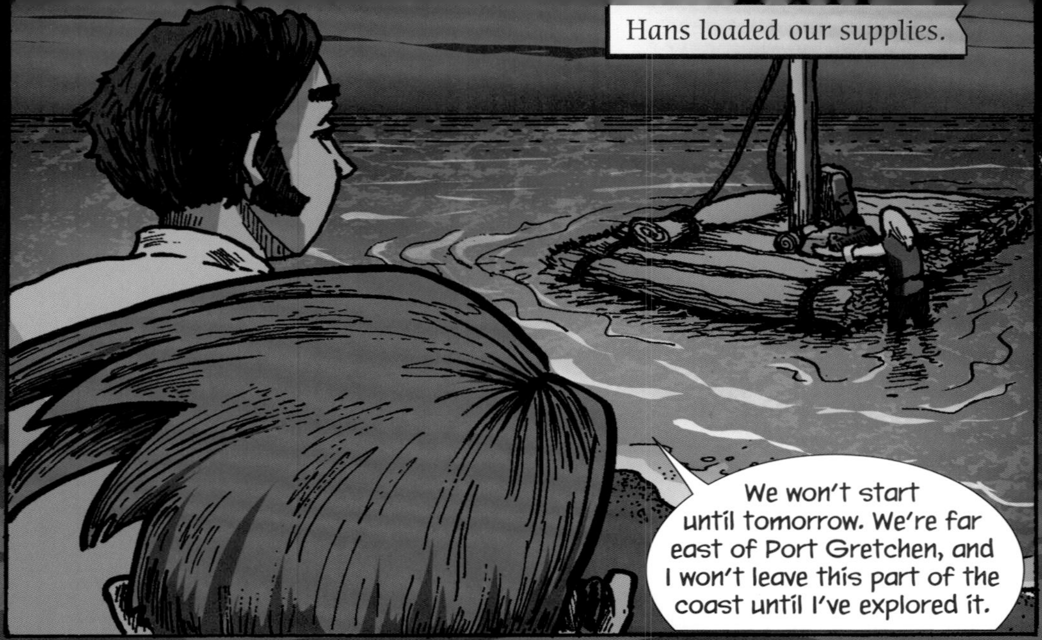
Hans loaded our supplies.
We won't start until tomorrow. We're far east of Port Gretchen, and I won't leave this part of the coast until I've explored it.

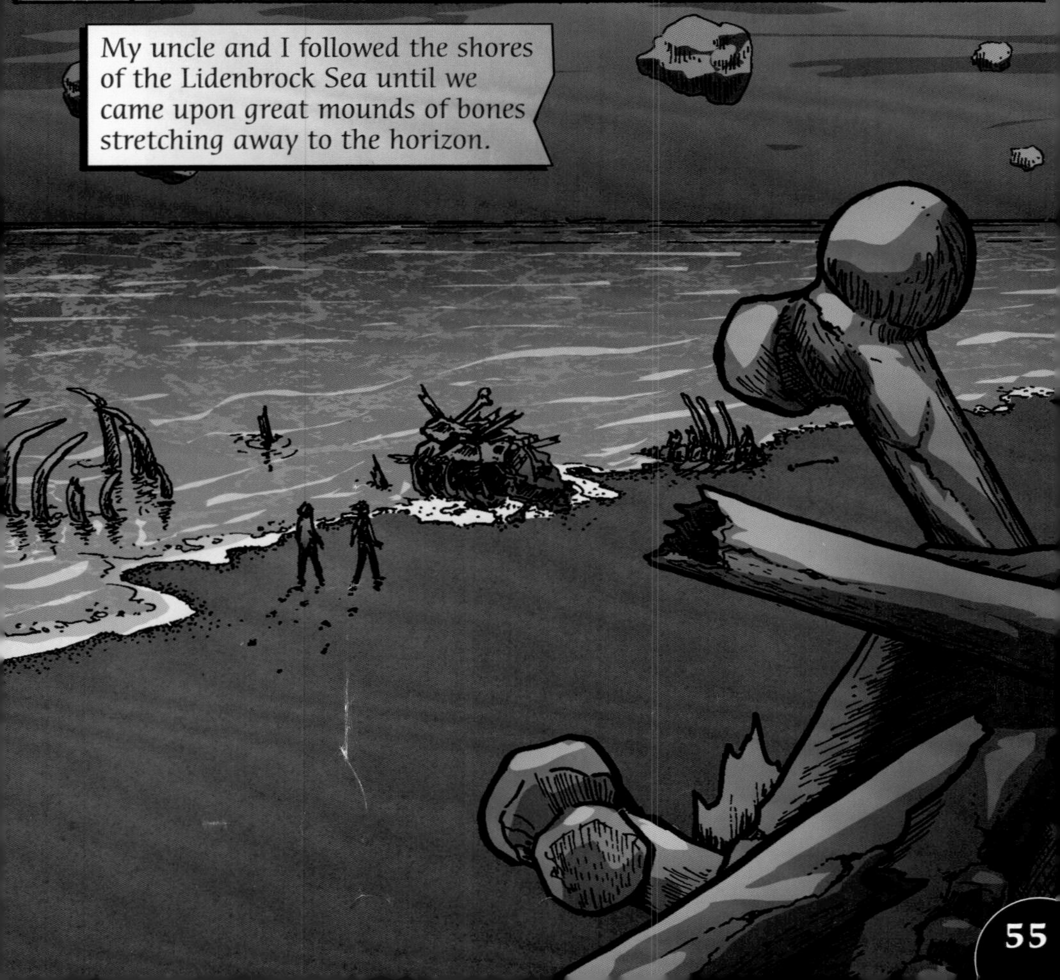
My uncle and I followed the shores of the Lidenbrock Sea until we came upon great mounds of bones stretching away to the horizon.

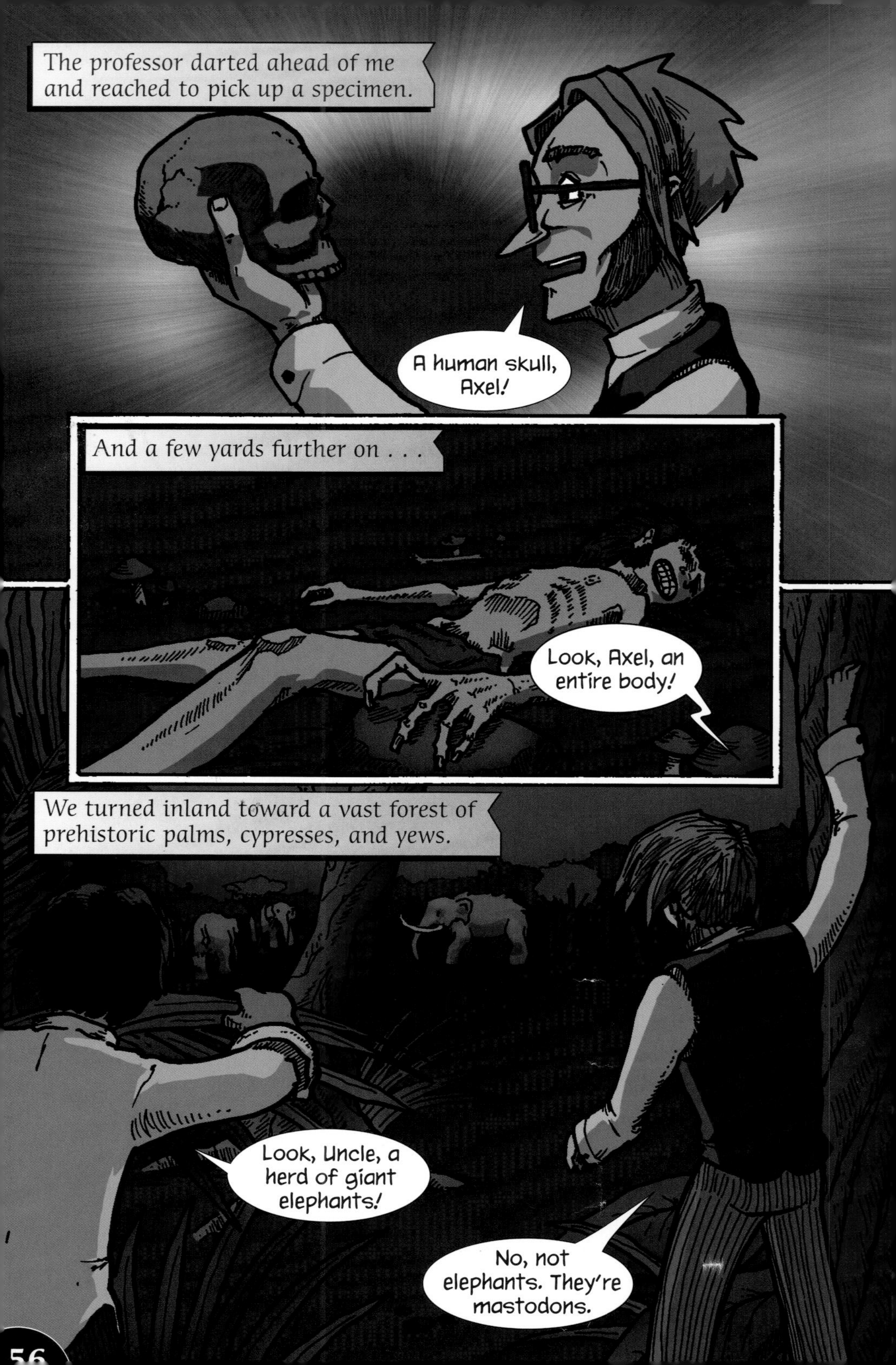
The professor darted ahead of me and reached to pick up a specimen.
A human skull, Axel!
And a few yards further on . . .
Look, Axel, an entire body!
We turned inland toward a vast forest of prehistoric palms, cypresses, and yews.
Look, Uncle, a herd of giant elephants!
No, not elephants. They're mastodons.

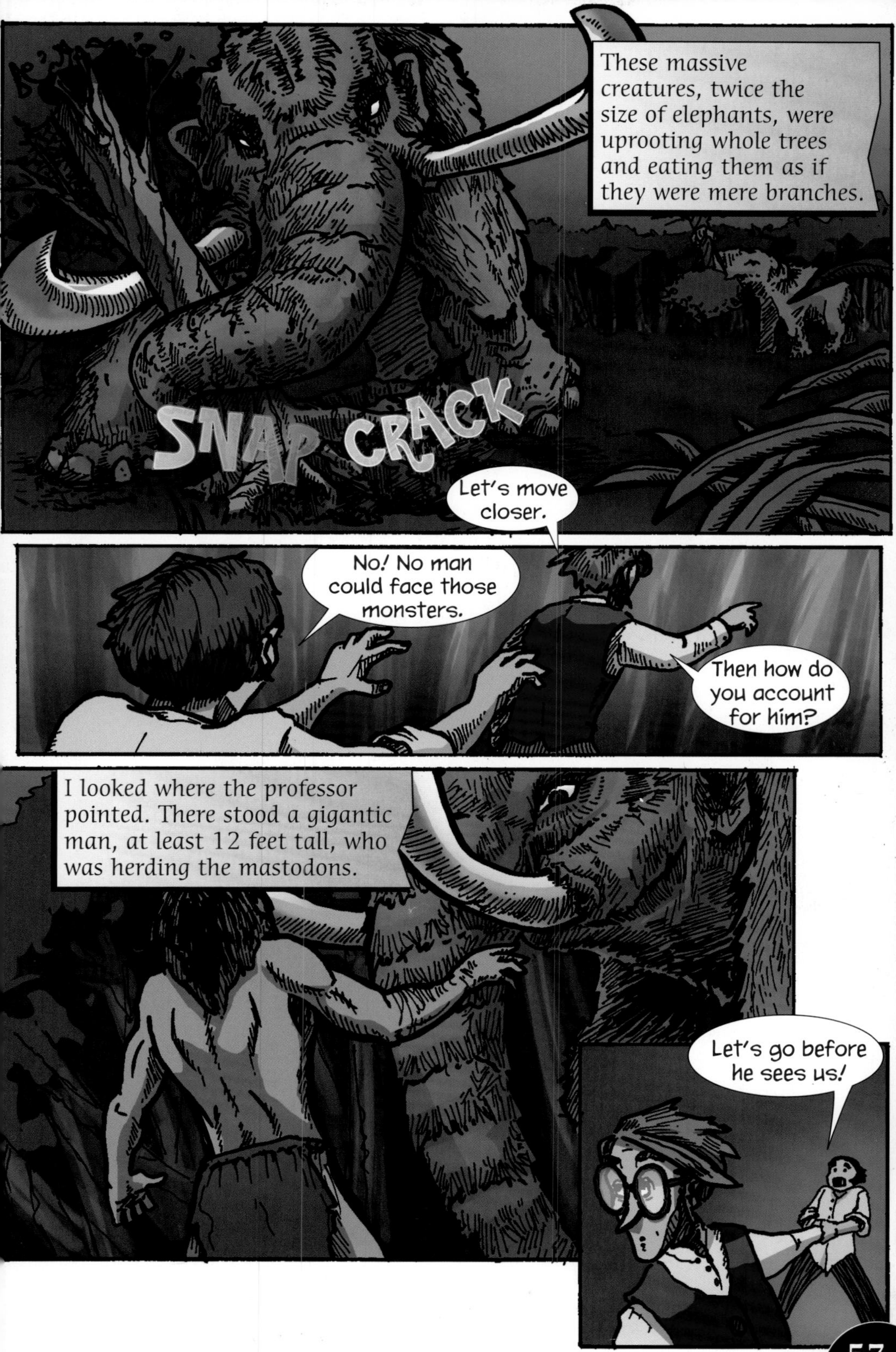

These massive creatures, twice the size of elephants, were uprooting whole trees and eating them as if they were mere branches.
SNAP CRACK
Let's move closer.
No! No man could face those monsters.
Then how do you account for him?
I looked where the professor pointed. There stood a gigantic man, at least 12 feet tall, who was herding the mastodons.
Let's go before he sees us!

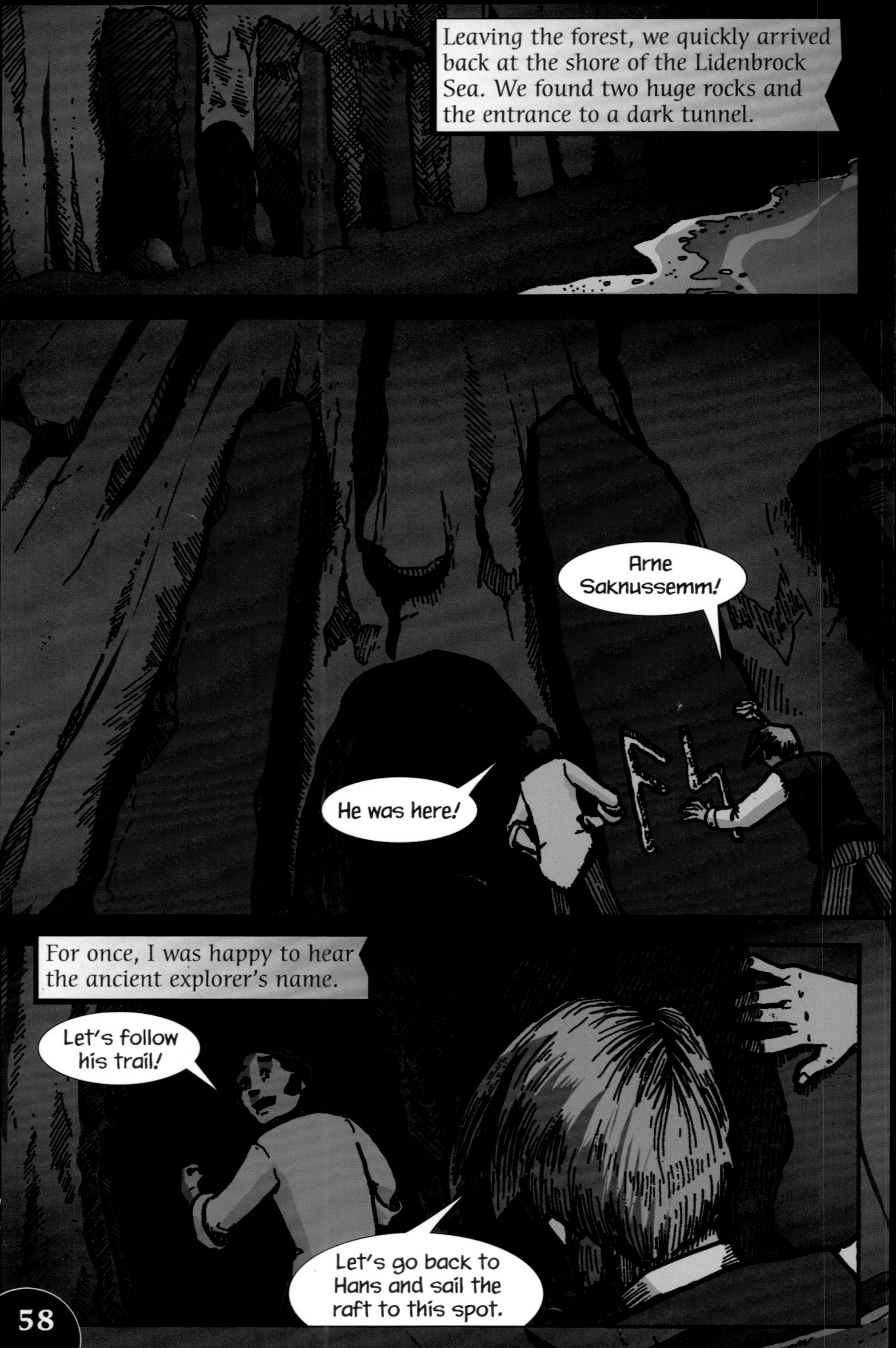
Leaving the forest, we quickly arrived back at the shore of the Lidenbrock Sea. We found two huge rocks and the entrance to a dark tunnel.
Arne Saknussemm!
He was here!
For once, I was happy to hear the ancient explorer's name.
Let's follow his trail!
Let's go back to Hans and sail the raft to this spot.

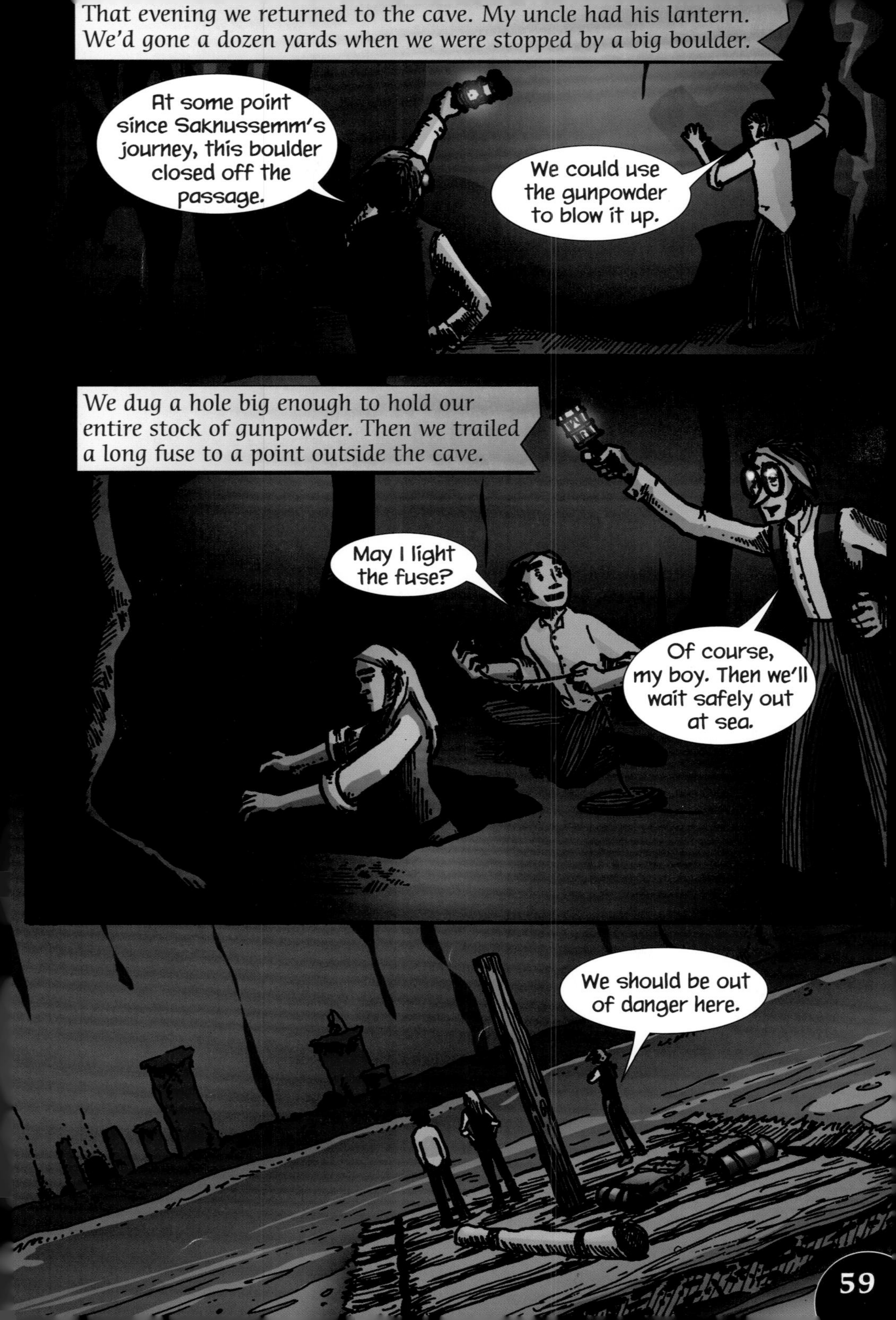
That evening we returned to the cave. My uncle had his lantern. We'd gone a dozen yards when we were stopped by a big boulder.
At some point since Saknussemm's journey, this boulder closed off the passage.
We could use the gunpowder to blow it up.
We dug a hole big enough to hold our entire stock of gunpowder. Then we trailed a long fuse to a point outside the cave.
May I light the fuse?
Of course, my boy. Then we'll wait safely out at sea.
We should be out of danger here.

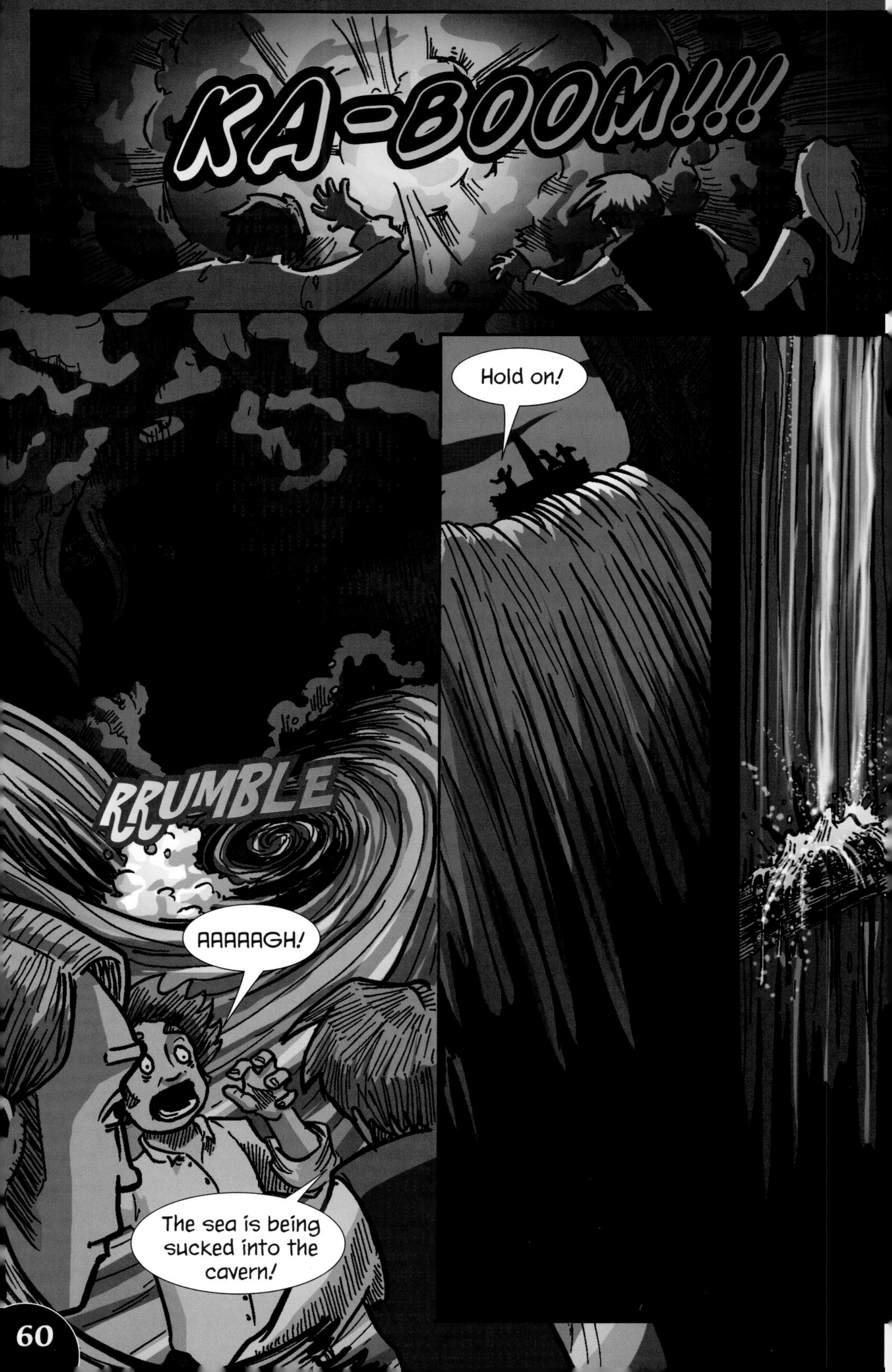
KA-BOOM!!!
RRUMBLE
AAAAAGH!
The sea is being sucked into the cavern!
Hold on!

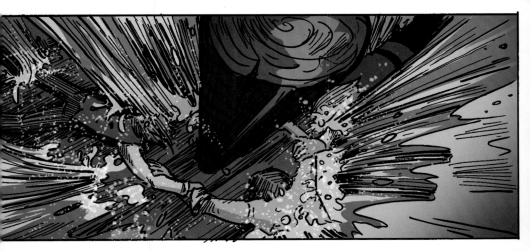

We're going up!

We were, indeed, heading up, at an amazing speed!

The temperature was quickly rising. It must've been 120 degrees.

If we're not drowned or smashed to pieces, we'll be burned alive!

Where there's life, there's hope.

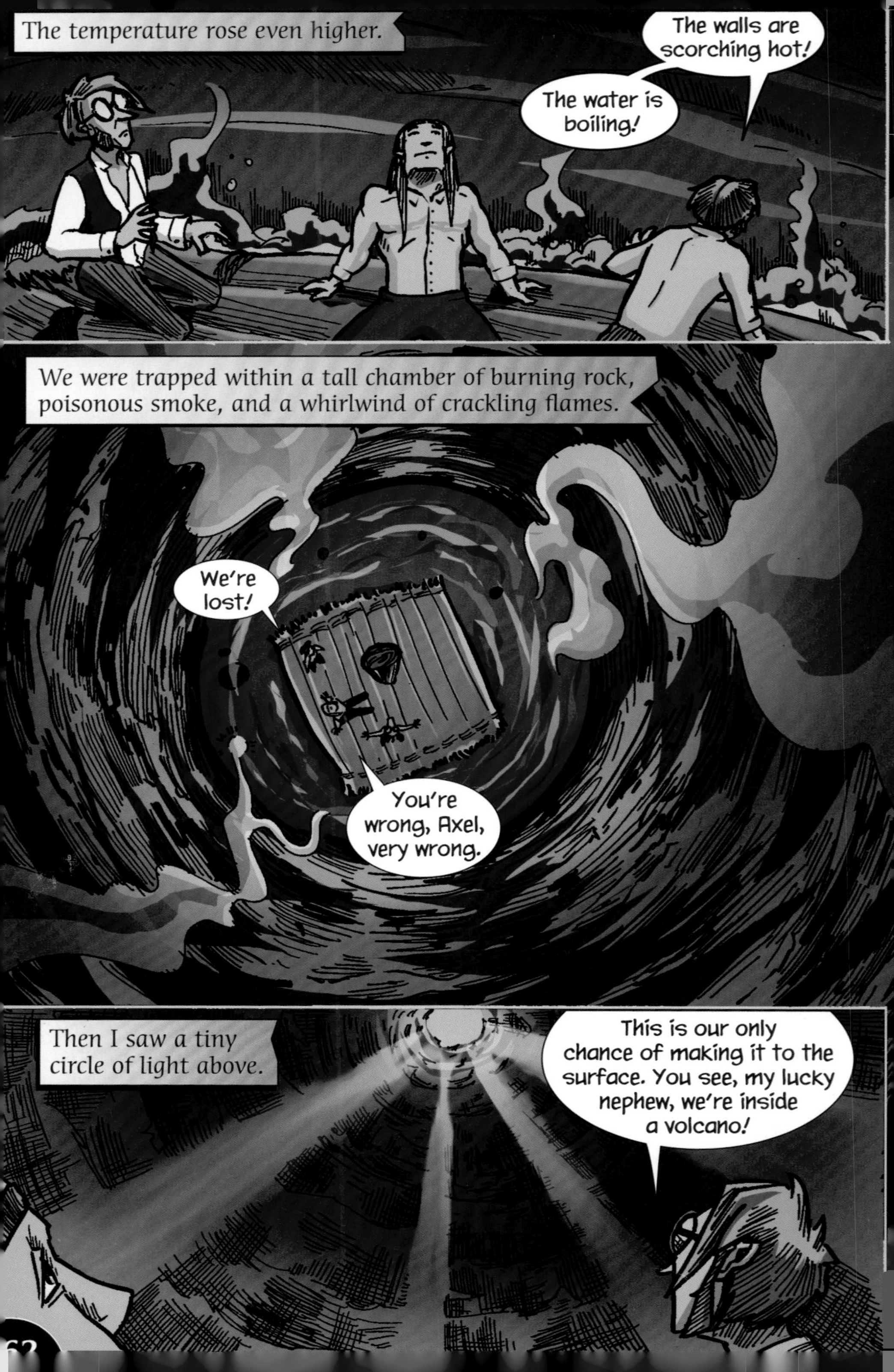
The temperature rose even higher.
The walls are scorching hot!
The water is boiling!
We were trapped within a tall chamber of burning rock, poisonous smoke, and a whirlwind of crackling flames.
We're lost!
You're wrong, Axel, very wrong.
Then I saw a tiny circle of light above.
This is our only chance of making it to the surface. You see, my lucky nephew, we're inside a volcano!

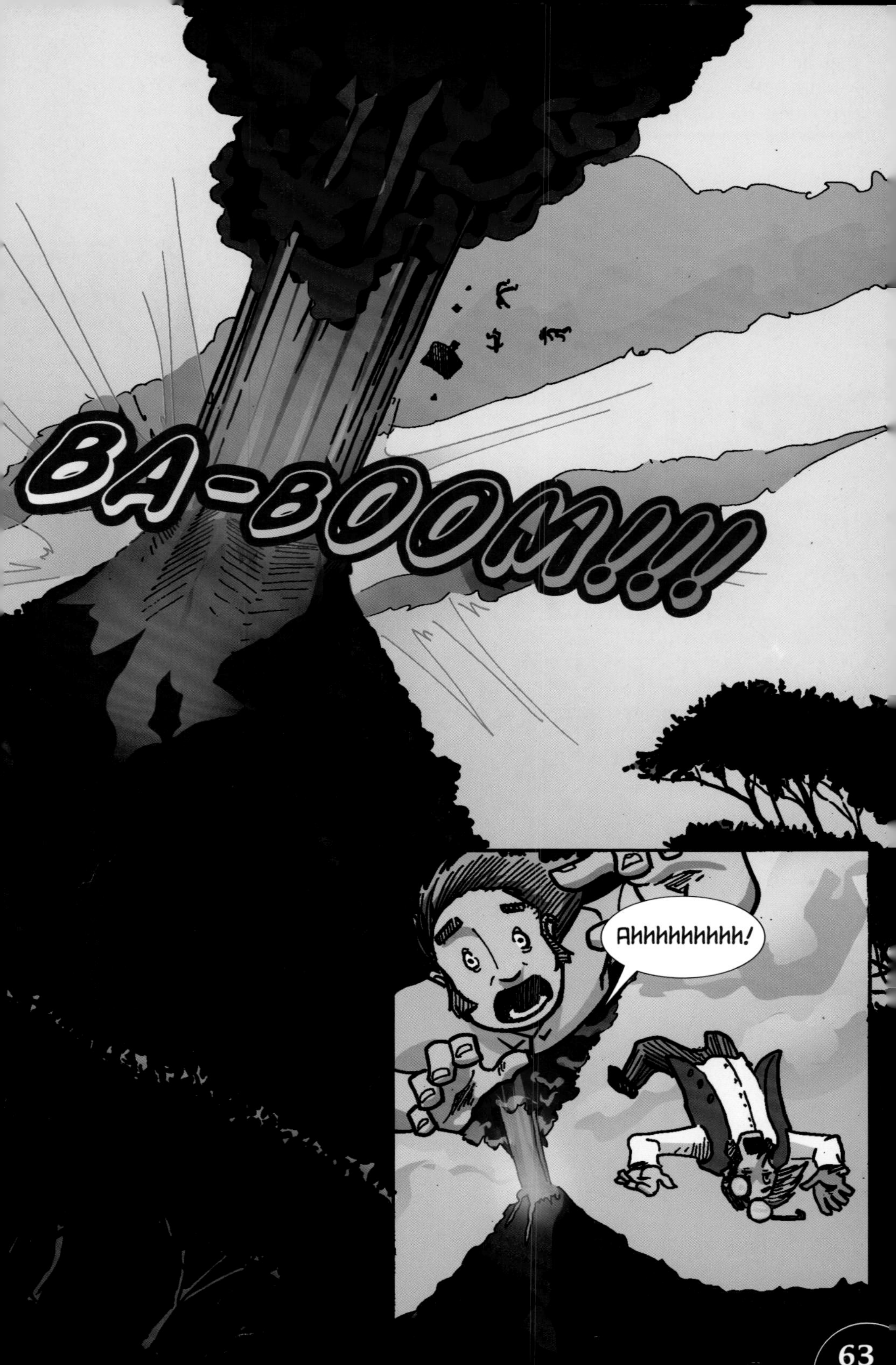
BA-BOOM!!!
Ahhhhhhhhh!

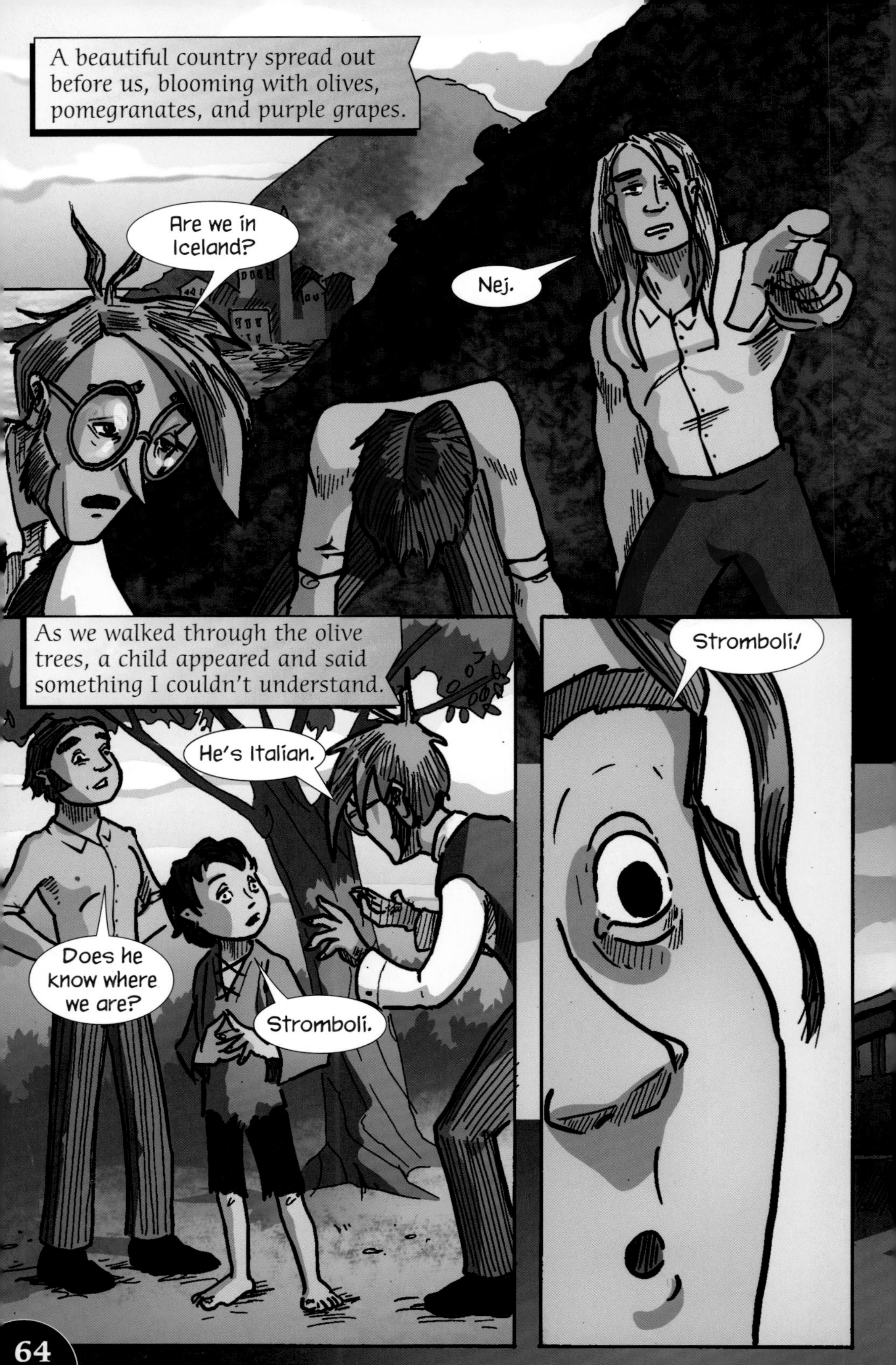
A beautiful country spread out before us, blooming with olives, pomegranates, and purple grapes.
Are we in Iceland?
Nej.
As we walked through the olive trees, a child appeared and said something I couldn't understand.
He's Italian.
Does he know where we are?
Stromboli.
Stromboli!

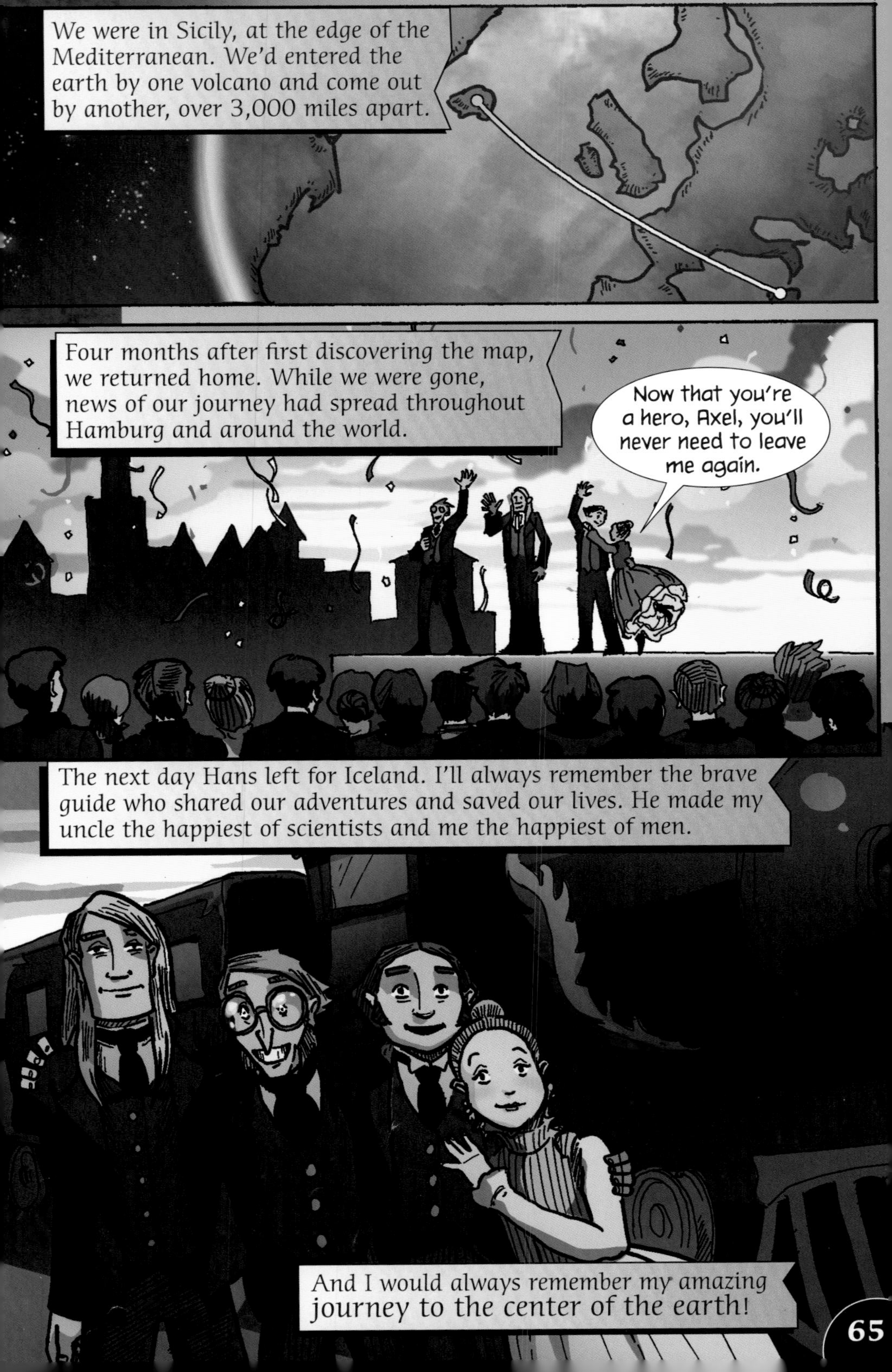
We were in Sicily, at the edge of the Mediterranean. We'd entered the earth by one volcano and come out by another, over 3,000 miles apart.
Four months after first discovering the map, we returned home. While we were gone, news of our journey had spread throughout Hamburg and around the world.
Now that you're a hero, Axel, you'll never need to leave me again.
The next day Hans left for Iceland. I'll always remember the brave guide who shared our adventures and saved our lives. He made my uncle the happiest of scientists and me the happiest of men.
And I would always remember my amazing journey to the center of the earth!

ABOUT JULES VERNE

Jules Verne was born on February 8, 1828, in France. Growing up near a river, the constant sight of ships sparked his interest in travel. As a young man, Verne even tried to run away and become a cabin boy. Fortunately, his father caught him, and soon Verne was off to study law in Paris. While there, Verne escaped the boredom of his studies by writing stories. When his father found out about this hobby, he stopped sending money for school. Verne started selling his stories, many of which became popular, including *Journey to the Center of the Earth* in 1864. Before he died in 1905, the author bought a boat and sailed around Europe.

ABOUT THE RETELLING AUTHORS

Davis Worth Miller and Katherine McLean Brevard are a married couple living and working together in North Carolina. They are both full-time writers. Miller has written several best-selling books. He is now working on a memoir and on several novels with his wife.

ABOUT THE ILLUSTRATOR

Greg Rebis was born in New York, but grew up mostly in central Florida. After working in civic government, pizza delivery, music retail, and proofreading, he eventually landed work in publishing, film, and graphics. He currently lives and studies in Rhode Island and still loves art, sci-fi, and video games.

GLOSSARY

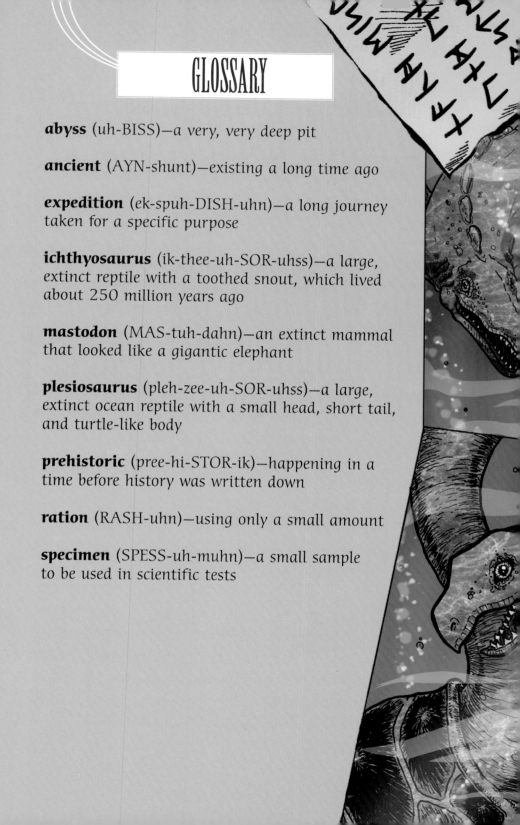

abyss (uh-BISS)—a very, very deep pit

ancient (AYN-shunt)—existing a long time ago

expedition (ek-spuh-DISH-uhn)—a long journey taken for a specific purpose

ichthyosaurus (ik-thee-uh-SOR-uhss)—a large, extinct reptile with a toothed snout, which lived about 250 million years ago

mastodon (MAS-tuh-dahn)—an extinct mammal that looked like a gigantic elephant

plesiosaurus (pleh-zee-uh-SOR-uhss)—a large, extinct ocean reptile with a small head, short tail, and turtle-like body

prehistoric (pree-hi-STOR-ik)—happening in a time before history was written down

ration (RASH-uhn)—using only a small amount

specimen (SPESS-uh-muhn)—a small sample to be used in scientific tests

MORE ABOUT EARTH'S CENTER

The author, Jules Verne, imagined the earth's interior was filled with rivers, oceans, dinosaurs, and giant mushrooms. Scientists, however, believe the center of our planet is made up of even more amazing things!

Think of the earth as an egg. An egg has three parts: the shell, the egg white, and the yolk. The earth also has three main layers: the crust, the mantle, and the core.

The Crust
Just like the shell of an egg, the crust is the hard, outer layer of Earth. It is also the thinnest layer. Beneath the oceans, the crust is only about 6 miles thick. The crust is made up mostly of rocks, such as granite and basalt (buh-SALT).

The Mantle
Underneath the crust is the thickest layer. At about 1,800 miles thick, the mantle makes up nearly 80% of Earth. This layer is extremely hot as well. So hot, in fact, that much of the rocky material has melted into liquid!

The Core
Earth's core has two parts: the outer core and the inner core. Both sections contain iron and nickel. In the outer core, these elements melt into liquid as temperatures approach 10,000 degrees Fahrenheit. Despite even hotter temps, the inner core remains solid under extreme pressure. This solid ball is about the size of the Moon!

Scientists use high-tech equipment to make predictions about Earth's center, but they've never actually been there. In fact, the deepest hole ever drilled is only 7.6 miles into the crust. The center of Earth is more than 3,800 miles beneath our feet! If we think of the earth as an egg, our deepest hole would just scratch the egg's shell.

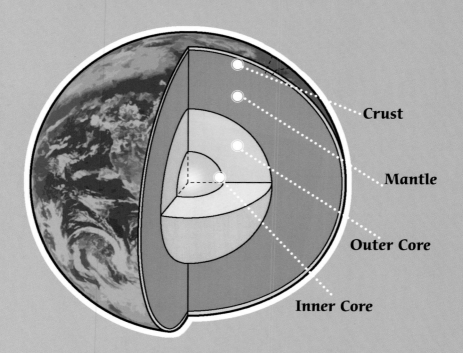

Crust

Mantle

Outer Core

Inner Core

DISCUSSION QUESTIONS

1. Each of the explorers had different skills that helped the group survive the journey. Name at least one skill for each character. Who do you think was most important to the group's survival? Why?

2. Axel, Uncle Lidenbrock, and Hans nearly ran out of water. Instead of returning to the surface, they took a risk and continued their journey. Are all risks good? Think of an example of a good risk and a bad risk.

3. At the end of the story, we find out that Axel and Uncle Lidenbrock never returned to the center of the earth. Why do you think they never went back? Would you have gone back? Explain your answer.

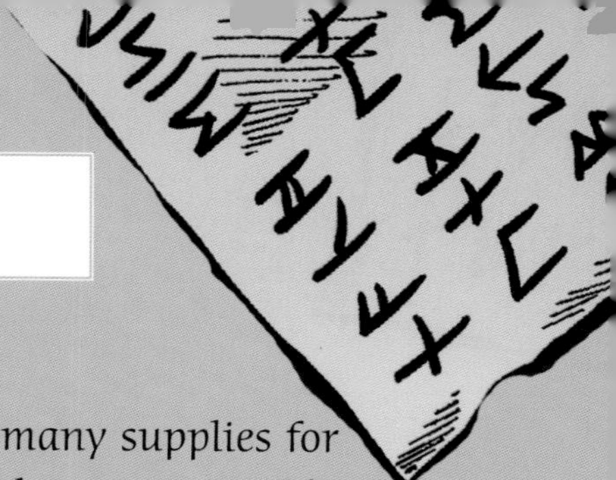

WRITING PROMPTS

1. The explorers in the story bought many supplies for their journey. Still, they almost did not survive. If you were taking the same journey and could only bring three things, what would they be? Explain your choices.

2. Find a globe or a map of the world. With your eyes closed, point to a place on the globe or map. Wherever your finger lands, write an adventure story about how you would travel there and what you would find.

3. Sometimes authors can't think of an idea for a story. If you ever have this problem, try starting with a title. Write a story with the title *Journey to the Center of the Moon.* How will your characters get to the Moon? What will they find there?

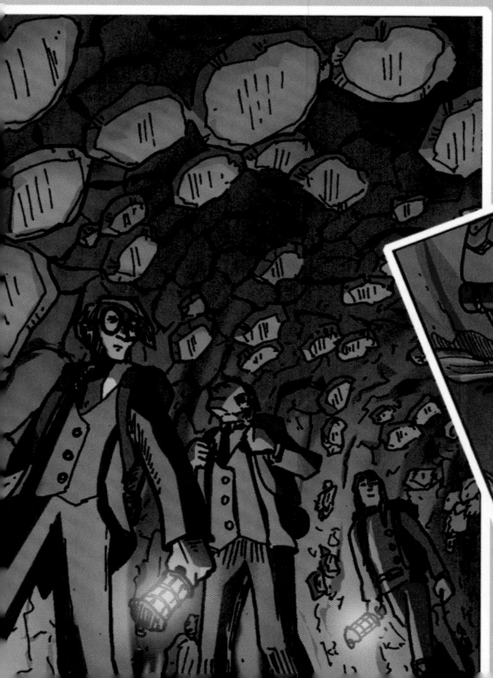

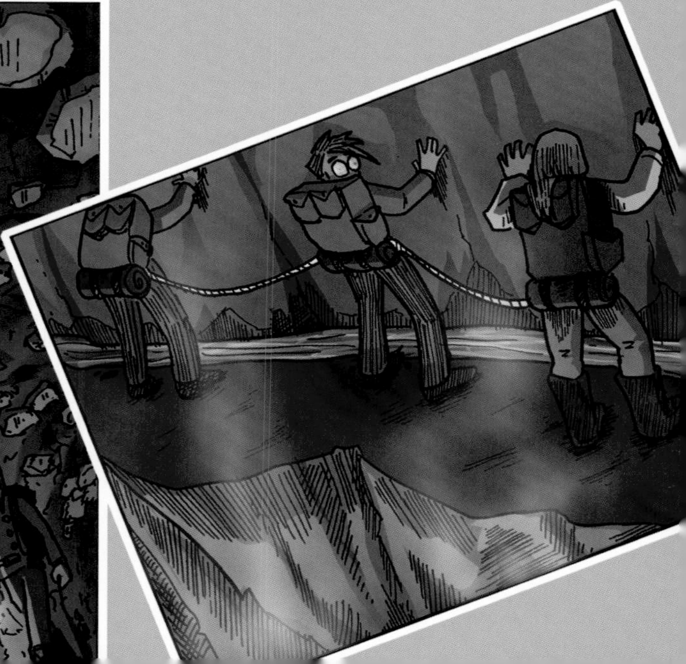

INTERNET SITES

Do you want to know more about subjects related to
this book? Or are you interested in learning about other
topics? Then check out FactHound, a fun, easy way to find
Internet sites.

Our investigative staff has already sniffed out great sites
for you!

Here's how to use FactHound:

1. Visit *www.facthound.com*

2. Select your grade level.

3. To learn more about subjects related
   to this book, type in the book's ISBN number:
   1598898329.

4. Click the **Fetch It** button.

FactHound will fetch the best Internet sites for you!